Praise for Johanna Sinisalo

Not Before Sundown
(a.k.a Troll: A Love Story)

'Blame global warming, but trolls are moving out of legend to scavenge at the outskirts of Finnish cities . . . Sinisalo's strange and erotic tale peers at the crooked world through a peephole. The troll comes to life after hours, unleashing glittering desires . . . Is the troll becoming more human (hurt, jealousy), or does he merely reveal our own trollishness?'
– *Guardian*

'Unsettlingly seductive . . . elegance, authenticity and chilling conviction'
– *Independent on Sunday*

'Chillingly seductive' – *Independent*, Best Reads of 2003

'A sharp, resonant, prickly book that exists on the slipstream of SF, fantasy, horror and gay fiction.' – Neil Gaiman

'An imaginative and engaging novel of urban fantasy . . . Overlapping narrative voices nicely underscore the moral of Sinisalo's ingeniously constructed fable: The stuff of ancient legend shadows with rather unnerving precision the course of unloosed postmodern desire.'
– *Washington Post*

'Simple but very powerful . . . A thoughtful, inspiring and rewarding work.' – *Gay Times*

'A wily thriller-fantasy . . . Each discovery sounds like the voice of a storyteller reminding us of how the gods play with our fates.'
– *The New York Times*

'A punk version of *The Hobbit* . . . Sinisalo cleverly taps the fabled legacy of myths while ditching the fairy-tale tone you might expect . . . Although the book exploits the conventions of the fantasy genre, it clearly transcends them . . . This smart, droll novel points out the absurdity of consumerism . . . [and] underscores how our ad-driven culture and its images permeate our lives.' – *USA Today*

'A brilliant and dark parable about the fluid boundaries between human and animal . . . Johanna Sinisalo creates scenes that make you laugh out loud; 10 pages later you're holding your breath with anxiety. Such talent is not to be taken for granted.' – *The Boston Globe*

'Sinisalo takes us on a brilliant and sometimes horrifying multidisciplinary adventure through biology and belief, ecology, morality, myth and metaphysics, in a quest for a wild place where trolls can run free.' – *Creative Loafing*

'Sinisalo uses the relationship between man and troll to examine the hidden motivations in human-human interactions . . . Sinisalo sets up thematic connections between nearly every event in the book, but she handles them with a light touch . . . this would be Ibsen's *The Wild Duck* – if the duck were the main love interest. Granted, Ibsen's doomed waterfowl never ended up in a pair of designer jeans, but both creatures highlight the uneasy role of feral nature trapped within civilized humanity.' – *Village Voice*

'While trolls in legends and stories often resemble werewolves, changelings and demons, in Sinisalo's book it's the humans whose beastly qualities are familiar and threatening. Her in-translation language is marvelous, sexy, enticing . . . Blood and bone mixes with unique humor and wit.' – *San Diego Union Tribune*

'Johanna Sinisalo has created a strange, beautiful tale, expertly translated, and cinematic enough for movie scenes . . . Thought-provoking, uniquely imaginative, and brimming with circus-sideshow details. . . Sinisalo's story ascends to more than just a freakish attraction by being intellectual and darkly comic all at once. The result is simply brilliant.' – *San Francisco Bay Reporter*

'Told as a modern-day fairy tale . . . haunted me long after I finished. It has all the elements, including some of the disturbing ones, found in so many of Grimm's stories, but is nonetheless a truly original novel.' – *Powells.com*

'Offers an ingenious dramatization of the nightmare of blurred boundaries between species, and a disturbing dystopian vision reminiscent of Karel

Capek's classic *War with the Newts*. A fascinating black comedy, from a writer who has made the transition to literary fiction with a giant's stride.'
– *Kirkus Reviews* (starred review)

'A sexually charged contemporary folk tale . . . Sinisalo's elastic prose is at once lyrical and matter-of-fact . . . The troll brings out Angel's animal instincts, representing all the seduction and violence of the natural world.' – *Publishers Weekly*

'The comedy is irresistible, the pages turn themselves, carried along by the quicksilver of an unbelievably imaginative pen . . . Run to this book . . . An entertaining variation on the eternal confrontation between man and beast, the light and dark angels which live in all of us.'
– *Télérama* (Paris)

Birdbrain

'*Birdbrain* is a graphic examination of two very different people and a harrowing allegory of humankind's problematic relationship with the planet.' – *Guardian*, a *Guardian* Book of the Year 2010

'A lyrical and occasionally sinister odyssey second only to making one's own foray into the wilderness' – *Publishers Weekly*

'A startlingly good book' – John Clute, *Strange Horizons*

'A sense of lurking horror that will leave you troubled for weeks'
– Sam Jordison

Johanna Sinisalo was born in Finnish Lapland in 1958. She studied theatre and drama and worked in advertising for a number of years before becoming a full-time author, at first writing science fiction and fantasy short stories. *Not Before Sundown* (2000), her acclaimed first novel, won the prestigious Finlandia Award and the James Tiptree Jr Award for works of science fiction or fantasy that expand or explore our understanding of gender. Also known in Finland for her television and comic-strip writing, she has won the Atorox Prize for best Finnish science fiction or fantasy story seven times and has been the winner of the Kemi National Comic Strip Contest twice. In addition to novels she has written reviews, articles, comic strips, film and television scripts and edited anthologies, including *The Dedalus Book of Finnish Fantasy*. Her short story 'Baby Doll' was a Nebula nominee and Grand Prix de l'Imaginaire nominee in France, and it was published in the *Year's Best SF 13* anthology in the USA. Her work has been translated into twenty languages, including twelve translations of *Not Before Sundown*. Three titles are currently available in English, all published by Peter Owen: *Not Before Sundown*, *Birdbrain* and *The Blood of Angels*.

LOLA ROGERS is a Finnish-to-English literary translator living in Seattle. She holds degrees in Linguistics and Finnish Language and Literature from the University of Washington and trained and interned in translation at FILI Finnish Literature Exchange in Helsinki. She has contributed translations of fiction, non-fiction and poetry to a variety of journals and anthologies and has translated numerous novels, including *True*, by Riikka Pulkkinen, which was a Shelf Unbound best book of 2012, and *Purge*, by Sofi Oksanen, chosen as a best book of 2010 by the *California Literary Review*, the *Sunday Times* and others. Other translations include works by Pasi Jääskeläinen, Johanna Sinisalo and Rosa Liksom. She is a founding member of the Finnish–English Literary Translation Cooperative.

THE BLOOD OF ANGELS

Also by Johanna Sinisalo and published by Peter Owen

NOT BEFORE SUNDOWN
BIRDBRAIN

THE BLOOD OF ANGELS

Johanna Sinisalo

Translated from the Finnish
by Lola Rogers

PETER OWEN
London and Chicago

PETER OWEN PUBLISHERS
81 Ridge Road, London n8 9np

Peter Owen books are distributed in the USA and Canada by
Independent Publishers Group/Trafalgar Square
814 North Franklin Street, Chicago, IL 60610, USA

English-language edition first published in Great Britain 2014
by Peter Owen Publishers

Translated from the Finnish *Enkelten verta*
Original edition published by Teos Publishers 2011
English-language edition published by agreement with Johanna Sinisalo
and the Elina Ahlbäck Literary Agency, Helsinki, Finland

Cover artwork Hannu Mänttäri
Typeset by Octavo Smith Publishing Services

PAPERBACK ISBN 978-0-7206-1004-8
EPUB ISBN 978-0-7206-1312-4
MOBIPOCKET ISBN 978-0-7206-1330-8
PDF ISBN 978-0-7206-1332-2

A catalogue record for this book is available from the British Library.

This work has been published with the financial assistance of FILI –
Finnish Literature Exchange

This book has been selected to receive financial assistance from English PEN's
"PEN Translates!" programme, supported by Arts Council England. English PEN
exists to promote literature and our understanding of it, to uphold writers'
freedoms around the world, to campaign against the persecution and
imprisonment of writers for stating their views, and to promote the friendly
co-operation of writers and the free exchange of ideas. www.englishpen.org

Supported using public funding by
ARTS COUNCIL
ENGLAND

From the Earth the bee rose swiftly, On his honeyed wings rose whirring,
And he soared on rapid pinions, On his little wings flew upward.
Swiftly past the moon he hurried, Past the borders of the sunlight,
Rose upon the Great Bear's shoulders, O'er the Seven Stars' backs rose
    upward,
Flew to the Creator's cellars, To the halls of the Almighty.

                   – *The Kalevala*: verse 15, translated by W.F. Kirby

When the bee comes to your house, let her have beer; you may want to
visit the bee's house some day.

                                         – Congolese proverb

DAY ZERO

The queen is dead.

She's lying in the entrance hole, delicate, fragile, her limbs curled up against her body.

I would recognize it as the queen just by the elongated lower body and clearly larger size compared with the worker bees, but there is also a little spot of colour on her back – I marked this female with yellow last year when I placed her in the nest.

Much too young to die.

And why had she left the nest to begin with?

I squeeze a puff from the smoker into the hive, but the bees don't come crawling out. They should be languid, of course, fat and heavy with honey to protect from this imagined forest fire, but there's no movement at all at the entrance.

My heart is racing now. I put down the smoker and pry the roof off the nest with a hive tool. I put the roof on the ground and start lifting the honeycombs out of the box one by one and stacking them on top of it.

The workers are gone.

Every one of them.

Just a few individual hatchlings crawling over the honeycombs looking befuddled, baffled by the sudden flood of light from above.

A tight fist closes at the pit of my stomach.

It can't be. Not *here*, too.

I carefully pick up the queen and put her on the palm of my glove. There's no reason this particular nest should need a fresh queen. Sometimes the old queen is killed when a colony ends a generation, but even if there were a new administration it wouldn't cause the bees to desert the nest.

Are they swarming? No. I'm sure I would have noticed it if the colony felt crowded or larvae had appeared in the queen's combs. And even if the old queen had evacuated the nest with her escorts to make way for a new queen the nest would have been more or less the same, although the group would be a little sparser and younger at first. It's also an unusual time of year to swarm; that usually happens in early or mid-spring.

But I look carefully at the surrounding trees because I certainly don't want this to be what I fear it to be. In spite of my hope I don't see any dark splotch, its blurred edges abuzz, in the branches or treetops.

But they've gone somewhere. Vanished as if into thin air. Into non-existence.

The queen lies lightly on my gloved hand like a flake of ash, but she feels so heavy that my wrist trembles. I take a breath, take the queen catcher out of my overall pocket and put the female inside. I drop the clip back into my pocket. Maybe I should send it to be analysed.

I don't dare to go to look at the other hives. Not now.

I'll do it tomorrow.

I have to take the rest of the frames out of this nest and put them in the centrifuge now anyway. Whatever it was that happened, the honey still has to be collected.

The sun is low over the meadow, soon it will be just an orange glow behind the tattered edge of the wall of spruce trees.

Back at the house I turn on the console with the remote. I hadn't wanted one of those voice-activated consoles with a monitor that covers half the wall; the screen on the wall over the table, smaller than the window, was big enough. There used to be a ryijy rug in that spot on the wall. The console is one Ari bought for me against my will, supposedly as a Christmas gift, me a grown man who supports himself, as if I were a spoiled child. A gift has to be something new, something expensive and useless, to keep your offspring content. I guess there was no way to avoid it, although it looks oversized in a little two-room cottage. Now that I've finally got used to it they tell me I ought to get a new one. Eero gave my console a nickname to tease me. He calls it my Lada, and sends me links to new fully interactive, high-definition models with the highest available data speeds. As if I needed the most advanced technology possible to watch the news, read my email, do my banking, order groceries twice a week and watch an occasional movie. Oh well – I do read Eero's blog on the console once in a while. It's almost like chatting with my son without needlessly disturbing him.

He's one to talk – Eero wouldn't have a wall console if you gave it to him for free. He carries a phone in his shirt pocket, does his work with a real computer with just the software he needs and doesn't even have an entertainment terminal. Even when he visits here he doesn't so much as glance at my console. He'd rather sit in the corner with his phone in his hand, wandering around the web looking at television shows and movies the way I would read a book.

It just so happens that the first message on my list is from Eero. Just a routine message to let me know he's still alive, some scattered comments about how he is, but his messages always warm me. There's some news, too. He has a paying customer now, a temporary gig sprucing up the customer feedback page for an electric-bicycle company. He'll be able to pay his rent for several months now.

I'm proud and embarrassed at the same time. I agreed to let him move to Tampere 'on a trial basis' on the condition that he kept his grades up and paid his own expenses. I had thought that a seventeen-year-old boy would come back to Daddy on the first milk train even if it meant an hour's commute to school. But no, Eero not only raised his grades – his prospects for the graduate-entrance exams in the spring are looking frighteningly good – he also succeeded in getting a job. At first he worked as a dishwasher and janitor at a vegetarian restaurant owned by an acquaintance, but now his contacts and capability in the world of the free net have started to provide employment. I send a short reply to his message. I can't resist mentioning that school is starting again soon and it has to come first.

Another message is from a courier company informing me that

the new bee suit I ordered from a bee-keeping supplier has arrived and has to be picked up at the service point in town. They used to call it the post office. It costs extra to get them to bring it all the way to my house, but picking it up isn't any particular trouble. It gives me an errand to do someplace other than work and is, in fact, a rare opportunity to run into people going about their ordinary business.

There's a pitch-thick, stone-cold irony in the fact that my new overalls arrived today of all days; a lot of joy it's going to give me if . . .

Hush. I had to order it, I really did. In spite of washings my old suit has become so saturated with honey that the bees are going to start to think my smoker and I are just a mobile, eighty-kilogram hunk of honey that needs to be brought safely out of fire danger.

A click of the remote and the news appears on the monitor. The top story is from North America, as it has been for a couple of months. The situation, already critical for a long time, has once again exceeded the most pessimistic predictions.

Twenty years ago, when the first wave of Colony Collapse Disorder arrived, I read reports about it with more worry than I'd felt since the days of the Cold War in the 1960s. Back then I was a little boy lying awake in bed waiting for a nuclear war to start. Now I can hear the clock ticking down to Judgement Day again.

I mentioned the disappearance of the bees to a random acquaintance back in 2006. I brought the subject up mostly to ease my own worried mind.

The acquaintance said it really was awful, but he supposed he'd just have to learn to live without honey.

Honey.

Food riots are continuing all over the USA and now they're spreading to Canada, too. The US government has once again limited the distribution of certain food products and in some states – mostly those that don't have their own source of potatoes – they're serving 'vitamin ketchup' along with the cornmeal mush and pasta in the schools because symptoms of malnutrition are starting to appear. Of course, it's nothing like real ketchup because there aren't any tomatoes.

The price of food has quadrupled in a very short time. Not long ago the American middle class was barely keeping up with the cost of mortgages, petrol, healthcare and tuition. Now they can't afford food any more.

The world's former leading grain exporter is reserving its crops to feed its own people, and the trade balance has plummeted. International credit is in shreds. With the rise in food prices, inflation is rampant. The EU banks and International Monetary Fund are making a joint effort to create at least some semblance of a buffer so that the US crisis doesn't completely collapse the world economy, which is already in turmoil. The dollar is on artificial respiration while we wait for the situation to 'return to normal'.

California's complete collapse is relegated to the second news item because it's already old news, but that's where the situation is worst.

Groups of refugees are invading the neighbouring states of Oregon, Arizona and Nevada as well as Mexico. Those south of the US–Mexico border are finally glad to have the wall the Americans once built, with its barbed wire and guard towers. It's coming in handy now that hungry, desperate fruit-growers are trying to get into Mexico to find any work they can get as janitors, pool boys, nannies and drug mules.

They're looking for someone to blame. The newsreader says that in 2004 the George W. Bush administration – making use of the media overload covering the approaching election and the war in Iraq – raised the 'tolerances' for certain pesticides. Since the media was too busy to take up the subject, the public was unaware of it, including bee-keepers.

Fruit-growers, however, must have known that their pesticides had a new kick and rubbed their hands in glee. But no one really knows if those pesticides are the cause of the disappearance of the bees or if it's something completely unrelated.

They have to find someone to blame. Someone has to pay. With the trees no longer bearing any fruit there's nothing left to live on.

A group of California orchardists is surrounding the White House now, furious and determined. 'Who killed the country?' is one of the most popular slogans on the demonstrators' signs. I notice another one: 'The CCCP didn't put us on our knees, the CCC did.' There seems to be some kind of riot outside the frame of the picture because I can hear noises that couldn't be anything but gunshots.

Next is a documentary clip from California.

Before the CCC phenomenon almonds were California's single most valuable export crop, more valuable even than Napa Valley wines, says a soft workmanlike voice, and a picture of February's blooming almond trees comes on the screen. The trees stretch for kilometres in every direction. Some sixty million trees in all, in even, orderly rows. Beautiful and sterile.

The picture shifts to China. The unregulated use of pesticides killed all the bees in Northern Szechuan province in the 1980s. It was an important fruit-producing region, and the livelihoods of the local people were entirely reliant upon what their trees produced.

Old footage comes on the screen – Chinese families right down to the grandparents climbing in the trees touching the blossoms with fluffy tufts on the ends of bamboo poles. They had, with great difficulty, gathered the pollen of the male flowers into basins, and now the screen showed them balancing awkwardly on ladders distributing the pollen to the female flowers. I watched their futile efforts with fascination. One single bee colony can pollinate three million flowers a day.

At the time they could hold out the hope of hand-pollination because labour was relatively cheap in Szechuan and it was only in that one area, the narrator explains. But now CCC has finally struck the USA and no amount of resources is enough to hand-pollinate all the fruit trees in California. Even if workers could be found it would cost billions in rapidly declining dollars. There's a rumour that the USA plans to reform their criminal sentencing to require community service in fruit-growing regions. Volunteers are being organized and trained in hand-pollination.

There are a few odd pollinating insects in California's almond orchards – the occasional fly or bumble-bee – but most of the almond harvest has been lost.

The correspondent restates the event: Colony Collapse Catastrophe, the Triple-C, BeeGone, hive desertion – more complete, widespread and destructive than any bee disappearance to date.

In the first half of the 2000s the abbreviation for the wave of hive desertions was CCD, Colony Collapse Disorder. They never found an air-tight, unequivocal explanation for it, just numerous theories.

No one's talking about a disorder any more. They talk about a catastrophe.

Almonds.

I remember seven years ago, when Eero spent a whole week at a summer camp in Lapland. I had some time on my hands. On a momentary whim I took a cheap flight to Malaga and rented a bicycle. I went on a leisurely ride around Andalusia and Granada, stayed in little village hostels, even took a side trip to the Alpujarras, along the mountain range. I stopped to wonder at the trees with their pale-green, hairy, tapering fruits the size of birds' eggs. Someone told me they were almonds. Inside the fruits were stones like in a plum, and inside the stones were the edible, delicious seeds.

The flanks of those Alpujarras foothills were filled with gnarled old almond trees. There were scores of them, and the fences around the orchards were invariably hung with glum, swaying, hand-painted signs that read 'Se Vende'. For Sale. The lifeblood of the Spanish highlands from time immemorial hadn't been profitable for some time. But now I can imagine the hordes of developers driving from village to village in their black SUVs offering rustling euros for those unproductive pieces of land. Toothless old men and stooped women finally owning something somebody wants, something sought-after, valuable.

And over it all, cheerful and diligent, waving her invisible baton, dances sister bee.

Before the Mediterranean countries got their production to rise, an almond for the Christmas pudding might be the single most expensive purchase for a holiday meal. And just as I'm thinking of a Christmas table I realize that the association with Christmas hasn't just come from the recesses of my mind. I can see something out of the corner of my eye, through the window. A flash of blue light over the Hopevale facility, harsh flashes like Christmas lights gone mad in the middle of an August evening. And then I hear distant noises, a shout, and I realize that the light is coming from the roof of an emergency vehicle.

SHOUTING TO THE POLICE FOR HELP

Once more my eye has fallen on a news item about whaling laws being openly and flagrantly broken. They're wiping the bloody points of their harpoons on the paper the international agreement's written on and laughing their heads off.

Whale meat is a luxury item that no one really needs. Although I do feel sympathy for those few Inuits who want to follow the whaling traditions and diet of their ancestors, I would prohibit them from whaling as well.

When pirates threatened merchant vessels and pillaged cargos in the waters off the Horn of Africa, mine-carriers and battleships were sent from all over the world. Piracy and lawlessness shouldn't be tolerated, of course, even if it's motivated by hunger and misery.

When intelligent creatures who are an integral part of marine nature and are no threat to anyone are being hunted to extinction – an extinction that no effort can ever reverse, unlike the loss of the trivial cargo of those freighters – the most you see is Greenpeace's rickety vessel when there's every reason to have a couple of real, authoritative-looking battleships with UN flags flying to announce that they'd better let go of those harpoons if they don't feel like going for a little swim.

Why is the protection of property so self-evident, so obvious, while giving other creatures their right to live is so difficult and complicated?

The argument over animal rights, or the lack thereof, is exactly like the argument we had long ago about the supposed inferiority of the non-white races. Or women.

That they may have seemed like thinking creatures, but what looked like intelligence was just a product of instinct, mimicry, a lower order of nature's creation striving towards our own image. At best we might concede that they were some sort of noble savages with a certain kind of cleverness, even almost a glimmer of a soul. But women and black-skinned people weren't really worthy creatures. Slavery and misery were all they were fit for because they didn't really suffer. The laments that came out of their mouths meant less than the whine of a kicked dog because dogs could at least be valuable, useful.

A day will come when people will cringe at the thought that their forefathers ate birds, other mammals and the people of the sea without regret. To them this will sound as barbaric and revolting as the fact that some primitive human populations ate members of their own species is to us.

Everything happens a step at a time. Defenders of oppressed groups will emerge from the ranks of those that hold power, first a few then more, until no one in any civilized country will say publicly any longer that feeling, thinking creatures shouldn't have rights and freedoms.

Already many people who still wolf down beef and pork without a care won't eat whale, dolphin, elephant or ape meat because so many sources tell us of these creatures' intelligence. Dolphins and primates have even been given their species' rights. In Spain they affirmed primates' right to life and freedom from torture and exploitation back in 2008.

But I don't know if anyone is policing that clause any more than they do the whalers.

LEAVE A COMMENT (total comments: 1)

USER NAME: Seppo Kuusinen
I agree that endangered species shouldn't be hunted. But where in the world are you going to draw the line once you start giving animals rights? Human rights are easy to understand because humans are a species that is conscious and behaves like a con-scious creature. Animals are more like machines or robots. Like computers, they react to the outside

world in complex ways, but there's 'nobody home'. They don't have language, science, art, technology or any kind of culture. Is there any evidence of their so-called intelligence? Where are their cathedrals and monuments? Animals have instincts and reflexes, but only humans make choices.

DAY NINE

I am a fleer from evil, a dodger of difficulty.

I could at least sometimes not avoid the things that I know are going to turn out badly or upset me or cause me extra trouble. How many times have I left an email unopened for days when I know the sender can't have anything pleasant to say to me (the tax man, Marja-Terttu), gone online to change my appointment for a check-up at the dentist that's already been put off too long, avoided looking at a stain on the shower wall that might be an omen of expensive and difficult-to-repair water damage?

This trait might make my choice of profession seem an odd one. But in my profession I don't make anyone upset or unhappy, not even myself. The tough, unavoidable part has already happened, and it's my job to take charge of the cold practicalities. I may not want to examine the stain on my own shower wall, but I would have no trouble answering a call about suspected water damage somewhere else and setting out with my toolbox swinging to make a house call and attest that it is, indeed, mould. You have a problem; I have a solution.

But unpleasantness, misfortune, wrongs that concern me I prefer not to face. It's a trait I no doubt share with the rest of the world. We prefer to put off inconvenient truths until the very last minute.

Maybe recent events are a sign that I've evaded and sidelined unpleasant realities so long that some cosmic cistern has finally been filled to the brim.

It's been nine days since I saw that one of the hives was empty.

Nine days since I saw the blue lights flashing at the Hopevale meat plant.

Things happen in bunches. Good fortune brings more good fortune, and bad luck is always followed by more of the same.

Going to the hives now is like knowing that the superpowers have been threatening each other for a long time, and they've set a time when the missiles will emerge from their silos if the other side doesn't submit to their demands, and now that deadline is at hand and I ought to turn on the television and see if the end of the world has arrived.

Almost everything I know about bees I learned from Pupa.

Pupa was there when my memories began, was already in his fifties, which in my eyes was a very old man. Pupa. I insisted on calling him that because it was somehow easier to say than Pappa – a pounding, almost mean-sounding word. He was already bald with liver spots on the top of his head like maps of undiscovered countries that I traced with my finger when I sat on the upper bench in the sauna and he sat on the lower bench taking a breather, grooves radiating from the corners of his eyes like the deltas of great rivers.

He had a name – Alpo – but I rarely remember it. Even on his death announcement it felt like the goodbye was for someone else, some substitute, a puppet representative.

When Ari (whom I, paradoxically, have never managed to call Dad) came to visit from America he always managed to mention to people who happened to stop in for coffee that in America Alpo is a brand of dog food. 'What are you, Dad, fifty-eight?' he would say. 'That's like eight hundred to you and me. You old dog.' He especially liked to say it when there were guests present and wink at me, implicating me in the joke, although I tried to look away, carefully balanced between my father and grandfather, not taking either one's side.

Then Pupa would usually go out to check the hives. He would always go out to the hives or find something to tinker with when anything upset him (like that tired dog-food joke) or weighed on his mind. 'I'm going out to the hives,' he would say, getting up in the middle of his coffee, leaving his cookie half eaten. 'Going out to the hives,' he would say, and the door would slam as he disappeared into the drizzly evening.

I often followed him. Pupa talked about his bees the way another person might talk about an animal that needed affection and grooming, like a horse that would get lonely out in the barn without regular visits from its master. A horse – maybe I thought of that because of the old-fashioned names Pupa used for the hives and their accessories. He called the removable inner box the bee pony. And the worker bees and drones were hens and cocks. 'Cocks, cocks', it reminded me of the noise when the hives caught May Disease, flight lameness. Spores had got into the honeycombs, and the bees came out of the hives in a group, fell down in front of it and bumbled and buzzed in the meadow grass, struggling vainly to fly. When you stepped on them they would make a sound like 'cocks cocks'. Pupa swore like mad, had to shovel the dead and dying bees from around the hive into a zinc bucket and dump them on the compost heap. The hives he burned.

The lameness was comprehensible; it was a disease, it had a cause, like dyspepsia or embryonic plague (Pupa used old names for diseases, too, and I'm sure he would be horrified at how many and multifarious the threats to the bees are nowadays). Diseases didn't empty the colonies completely like the bee collapse does, the hives a riddle like the *Marie Celeste*, that ship found on the open sea, empty, warm food still on the table, a parrot in the captain's cabin who no doubt knew what had happened but couldn't speak, at least not well enough or in a way we could understand.

Parrots.

They make me think of Eero.

Like so many things do.

Thinking of Eero sends an icy wave falling into the pit of my stomach, a horrible stab, and I gulp for breath, jerking the air into my lungs in long sobbing breaths.

There's nothing else I can do.

I go out to the hives.

EERO THE ANIMAL'S BLOG
PONDERINGS ON OUR RELATIONSHIP WITH ANIMALS

TO THE HONOURABLE SEPPO KUUSINEN

I'm responding outside of the comments section in the body of a post because the construction of your question demands closer inspection.

No matter how sophisticated and rational another animal species' behaviour may be we quickly label it as instinctive. We think of animals, in your own words, as meat robots, somehow programmed to blindly make their way from birth to death. We think that because we have tools and houses and works of art we're automatically creatures of a higher order with a right to control other life forms. We forget the sticks that birds use to dig grubs from holes in wood, the stones that sea otters use to crack open shellfish. Many birds' nests are not only woven and cushioned but also masterful works of creativity, decorative little Versailles, each one different.

(Besides which, recent studies such as this one support the idea that humans behave much more 'instinctively' than previously thought. Often our choices and decisions are made straight from the spinal cord, if you'll pardon the expression, and are rationalized in the brain only long after the fact. In other words, even if animals do act largely on 'instinct', so do people; so good luck finding any great difference in that department.)

But what about language – spoken language? Now there's something that definitely separates us from all the rest of creation – an insurmountable wall. Whale song, chimpanzees' expressively powerful use of calls and gestures, the pheromone communication of ants? Those are all just the feeble, involuntary outcome of nerve impulses, dictated by those famous instincts.

When we consider parrots' endearing quality of mimicking human speech we're apt to think of them as recording devices made out of flesh and feathers. Not really communicating.

But go ahead and think that. In one of Kurt Vonnegut's books there's a story of humans encountering creatures from outer space for the first time and the aliens happen to communicate by farting and tap-dancing. (Things don't go well for them, by the way.) But what if one of Vonnegut's aliens abducted you and put you in a cage in their living-room? After a few years wouldn't you start attempting some kind of primitive communication with your jailers? You would imitate them, repeat the most common expressions you picked up on, in an attempt to make at least some contact with the other species. In a few years you would be farting and tap-dancing in your cage, and the expressions of delight you received in return would make you try to learn more. You might not quite understand the meaning of what you were expressing, but you would definitely be *communicating.*

Language is often thought of as the dividing line between humans and animals. Only humans are able to convey complex, abstract information by means of language.

What about the dances of bees? It is language conveying refined, syntactic, vital information concisely and precisely. Bees convey direction, distance and mathematical quantities to their fellow bees with their movements.

Instinctive behaviour, say the Seppo Kuusinens of this world, because nothing can top our achievement of moving air with our tongues and vocal cords to send vibrations to the eardrums of other individuals – that's the only nuanced, meaningful, *real* communication.

So now that we've learned the practicality and 'instinctiveness' of the bees' dances, we're not the least bit interested in what the bees are saying to each other in the gaps between the exchange of information. Are they telling jokes? Swapping gossip? Hatching plots?

LEAVE A COMMENT (total comments: 1)

USER NAME: Blablabla
    Whatever. You really have to dig for human

characteristics in animals. A dog gives you his paw and suddenly he's intelligent, practically knows how to talk. And once we've 'found' these traits by forcing and twisting the facts we'll be able to start demanding that pigs and cows have a right to vote.

DAY NINE

I only have about a dozen hives. It's just a hobby. About four hundred kilograms of honey a year. Not enough to pay a minimum wage.

The hives are on a little rise in deciduous woods to the north-west of the cottage. The birches and aspen offer welcome shade in the summer, but when the bees start to wake up in the early spring the naked trees let the weak sunlight through and the bees are ready to venture out as soon as the temperature gets above zero in the warmth of the sunlight. There are also a lot of willows in the area, which are a vital early source of nectar.

I finally went today to pick up my new bee suit from the service point. I was intent on finishing my errand quickly, not stopping to chat, but no one wanted to anyway. I did notice some looks – wary, pitying, eyes delicately turned to the floor or the wall, people avoiding me, keeping their distance as if I had some nasty infectious disease. In my profession I've learned to understand such behaviour, but not directed at me.

The overalls feel a little loose when I put them on (I may have lost weight – don't even remember whether I've eaten anything) and are oddly stiff. I'm sure all new clothes feel that way before your body shapes them.

I know that my parading up and down, supposedly to test them out, my careful loading of bits of rotten wood into the smoker, are delay tactics, a way to put off finding out the answer to whether the end of the world has arrived.

At the first hive the smoker flushes out a sizeable swarm of lively bees. I pull off the roof of the hive, still holding my breath. Then I let my breath out as I look at the frames in one slow exhale, a sigh of relief. This colony is healthy and alert. The hive is almost ready to harvest; I could even extract the honey from a couple of frames and put some empties in their place, they've been so busy.

It was just one colony. I'm sure there are lots of things that could have thrown the bees' life out of kilter. Mice and other small mammals try to infiltrate the hives, usually in winter – how do I know it wasn't some little predator, maybe a shrew, braving the stings to get in and, even though it had fled, causing such a panic that the colony decided to abandon the hive. Maybe the queen just suffered some accident in the fracas.

If I cry wolf, and there's no wolf there, will I be believed when something bad really *does* happen?

After I've checked the bulk of the hives I'm reassured. The colonies are busy and full of life, the brood cells are buzzing with lively offspring, the combs so full of honey that I decide to swap some frames with empties to be filled. Although the season's almost over there's still plenty of willowherb and heather blooming. It's particularly lush in the woods east of Hopevale.

To be on the safe side I decide to empty the abandoned hive completely and disinfect it. Or burn it, just to be sure. It might be asking for trouble to try to install a new queen and colony in the abandoned box, even if the problem was simply some new mould or parasite. (Although in that case I ought to have seen sick and dead bees. *Ought* to have.)

I put the roof back on the last hive and extinguish the smoker. I'm heading back to the extractor room, counting in my mind how many empty frames I'll need, when something stops me like it's got my leg in its jaws. I jump, almost fall down, and I hear an ominous tearing sound. I grab the nearest hive instinctively to steady myself, and it rocks. I lose my balance.

Oh, no.

My brand-new bee suit has caught on a strip of wood nailed to one of the hives and used as a handle. I had walked too close to the nest in my absent-mindedness. When I look closely I see that the strip has warped as it has aged and is sticking out a millimetre from the edge of the box. The nail should have been hammered in closer to the end. Pupa had his careless days. And my overall pocket has caught on this unnoticed, cleverly placed trap. The seam is torn at the pocket and two centimetres down the leg.

It's not a large tear, but it's big enough for an angry bee to get in, so I leave quickly, covering the hole with my glove just in case.

Nine days ago I feared the world was ending, but it didn't end – or not in the way I expected. Then the new bee suit came, like a fateful irony, a meaningless object. Now I'm taking the rip in the suit too much to heart. It's the very first time I've worn it. Equipment shouldn't damage so easily – the suit is obviously a dud. At least the tear is right at the seam. I can patch it up myself. But if I want to put new frames in the hives I'll need a bee suit, so old faithful will have to be called into service again.

Luckily I haven't thrown it away. It's hanging in the hayloft.

I climb the ladder up to the trapdoor that leads to the loft. When Pupa's parents were young the door had been used to pitch hay straight down into the cow stalls, back when the old cottage I live in was the main building of Hopevale Farm. The two-cow barn is now used as a woodshed and storehouse. It was built a bit oddly, as an addition to the sauna, under the same roof – or maybe the sauna was an addition to the barn; I've never thought to ask. Maybe they thought that heating up the sauna a couple of times each week would make the cows on the other side of the wall a little more comfortable in winter. Pupa's father built a much larger barn at the time the new Hopevale farmhouse was built, but the cosy, steamy sauna was still used.

The hayloft is divided into two sections by a wall. The front is almost empty, just a few brown cardboard boxes with MARJA-TERTTU written on them. They're things she forgot that I've put together in one place, thinking I would send them on to her at some point. I never have, but I can't bring myself to throw them stuff out. And anyway, the loft is the final resting place for lots of things that have fallen out of use but are still in good condition and might come in handy some day. 'In case there's a war or a famine,' Marja-Terttu once said, oozing sarcasm.

She had no idea of her powers of prophecy.

*

31

There's a gap in the wall that leads to the back space, and there, under the sloped roof, is a collection of all kinds of things that might be needed some day. The 'junk room' Pupa called it. Stacks of old terracotta pots and a pitchfork with no handle and an old kitchen stool and a bent fish-trap and discarded but still perfectly serviceable clothes hanging from nails in the walls collecting dust, like my paint-stained overalls. And the honey-stiffened bee suit.

It's hanging on the junk room wall like a limp, white human form. I give it a shake with a flick of my wrist. Dust flies, even though it's only been hanging there for nine days.

I put it on in the centrifuge room. It immediately feels like a favourite pair of jeans. It's used to me. I don't really need to put new frames in the hives today, but it helps to do something, anything. And what else do I have to do when I'm on sick leave?

I go back out, light the smoker and notice from a distance that one of the stacks of hive boxes, the ones that are painted green, is oddly slumped. It's the same hive that tore a hole in my new suit. The catch and stumble has knocked it out of balance.

When I touch the top box the whole thing sways. Not much, but noticeably. I crouch down and examine the bottom of the hive. One of the bricks at the base, the one at the corner, of course, is crumbling a little. There's a thin, meandering crack that goes all the way through the brick. There must have been a hairline crack in it back when Pupa first put the bricks there as a base, and the winter freezes and summer changes in moisture have widened it until I stumbled against that one hive and the brick cracked and that half of the hive pressed into the ground a little. That was enough: the whole hive is out of balance.

I don't even consider trying to lift the hive and fix the base where it stands; now that the honey's starting to accumulate each box weighs quite a few kilograms. Nor do I want to start taking every frame out since I'll be collecting the honey soon in any case. But I'm reluctant to leave it out of alignment from now until autumn. I might bump into it again in passing, or a badger might come at night poking around for something sweet and knock the whole thing over.

If I try to move the broken brick out of the way and shove a new one in its place it should keep it stable at least until harvest time, maybe even until I get it ready for winter.

So all I need is a brick. Where did I put the ones from when the old main building was torn down? I took a dozen or so to keep – you can always use a brick here and there for small fixes.

In the junk room, where else? I remember it clearly; Ari tossing the bricks up to me from the barn, showing that he still had a strong arm when he needed it, chucking the bricks into the air with a laugh to cover his grunts while I bent over the edge of the trapdoor and caught them in my gloved hands. It was an exhilarating game for adults, both of us showing off our manhood. He had to let the brick fly high enough, at just the right angle for me to reach it, and I had to catch it effortlessly, as if it were as small and light as a ping-pong ball.

I take a deep breath because a vast hatred of Ari is starting to well up from somewhere deep within me again, vomiting up uncontrollably. I try to direct my thoughts to the bricks – bricks, bricks bricks, damn it – and it helps a little. I remember the exact place now; they're in a pile against the north wall of the junk room. I would have seen them when I went to get my bee suit if I'd known to look for them. If I'd known that I was about to need one.

I put them there carefully, maybe so I could preserve at least a small piece of the old Hopevale house, which was a home to me, unlike the stone mansion Ari has now. He ordered a majestic, prefab house and tore the old one down as soon as Pupa was under the dirt. Maybe he had his reasons – the old place was an unsightly 1960s house with a flat roof and grey cladding that was supposed to be weatherproof. Nobody worried about asbestos back then. Pupa left me the sauna and the cottage in his will, separating it off from the property so that I would also get the beehives. Ari was probably a little hurt by the way the inheritance skipped a generation, must have seen it as a rebuke . . .

No. Not now. I'm not going to think about Ari right now.

I'm thinking about bricks. Bricks, bricks, bricks.

Back to the hayloft. Move!

*

33

But I am thinking about Ari.

The time he came to visit Finland, in the summer of 1976 (before he came back for good two years later), I was fourteen. I was gangly, narrow-shouldered, morose, the mere beginnings of a man, peering out under a thin, shaggy fringe at this strange man who was as big and broad as a double bed. He was broad in his speech and in his deeds, too, laughed as broadly as anyone with at least a hundred teeth in his mouth.

He tried to get to know me again by shaking me by the neck, mussing my hair, elbowing me in the ribs, laughing his open-mouthed, American laugh that sounded almost idiotic to me at first. He invaded my personal space in a very un-Finnish way and bruised me inadvertently. Even the Levis he brought me from New York, the only real pair in the village, which should have made me incredibly proud, offended me. They were several centimetres too short and too big around the waist. In his mind's eye Ari had seen the chubby little boy of three years earlier, not me.

And when he gave Pupa the nickname Old Dog I was embarrassed. Pupa's name wasn't his fault, and neither was mine. From what I've heard it was Ari who wanted my name to be Orvo, after my mother, whose name was Orvokki. I didn't know and had never heard of another boy with that name. The only thing that assured me that it was even a real name and not some damned girl's nickname was a television show from my early childhood with a circus ringmaster named Orvo – a man, luckily. *The Parrot Circus* they called it. (Parrots again. Eero, I think, and shut my eyes from the sheer pain.)

I wouldn't even have been christened Orvo if my mother, Orvokki, hadn't died almost immediately after I was born of complications the nature of which remained vague to me and about which I never asked. But you can always find a kernel of levity in the sadness, if you want it badly enough. Ari managed to find it even in his wife's death – he called me Orvo the Orphan.

My moroseness wasn't long-lived, though. I started to see that Ari's ease, his spontaneity, were genuine; they were just so unusual in Finland at that time that you automatically assumed he was play-acting – the American clown. Even the fact that, contrary to custom, he would just touch me in way I was entirely unused to, seizing me by my skinny shoulders even in public places, putting his arm tightly around me and squeezing – started to change in my opinion into brave, manly behaviour. Ari dared to be different from other people, to march to his own drum, and the estrangement I felt faded, first in moments of acceptance, later in a budding admiration and, I might as well say it, love. At a certain point even his tired old joke about 'our old dog' started to have a funny, anarchic ring to it: here was a man brave enough to makes jokes even at his own venerable father's expense. And wasn't an observation like that – word play with another person's name – just a sign of his affection, and not really teasing? It was the kind of rough tenderness that ice-hockey players had when they ribbed each other in the locker room with those nicknames that seemed insulting on the outside but came from an affection on the inside. I decided that I would think up a clever nickname for Ari or a sarcastic joke about some characteristic of his and use it constantly. It would be our way of teasing one another, which he'd given me indirect permission to do.

To be completely honest, my shyness and prejudice about Ari were lifted a lot by the envious looks of the other boys in the village, their gazes lingering on my father's cowboy boots and leather jacket, not to mention the used Chevrolet he'd bought just to use while he was in Finland (and which he, perfectly Ari-like, washed, waxed and sold just before he left at a profit). And Ari gave me money. Whenever he came back from buying groceries he would pour all his change into my hand. 'It's just wearing out the bottom of my pocket,' he would say with a laugh.

The too-short Levis slid over my bony hips nicely. I cut the legs off above the knee and wore them as shorts. I refused to let my grandmother hem them, letting them unravel into fringe like a hippie. The waistband hung loose, almost below my budding naval hair, and Ari laughed and my grandma was aghast and Pupa smiled wickedly, but no one told me I couldn't wear them. That and letting my hair grow way past my ears was my way of rebelling, I guess.

Although I did have one other rebellion, now that I think about it: my choice of profession.

Ari wanted me to go to business school.

I tried to talk to him about bees. Pupa had taught me everything he knew about them, and I'd learned a lot more on my own. The hives would be Ari's after Pupa died because the land would be his – or that's what we thought before Pupa's will – and I needed his approval. I was thinking that the operation could be expanded. Broadened, modernized.

'But that's just a hobby, for heaven's sake,' Ari said. 'Some people grow a couple of potatoes for midsummer, some tinker with their cars. I have a few beehives. You can take care of them, but that's no profession for you. What's a bee compared to a bull calf?'

What indeed?

Once I was a little older and was chasing a teenage girl, the budding relationship wilted when she refused to come over to Hopevale. Because of the bees. Buzzing, bug-eyed, stinging monsters, who made up for their small size through the terrifying power of their sheer numbers. I have no doubt it would have been easier to get her to come over if my family had raised rattlesnakes. There was no point trying to explain the basic beauty and lovableness of bees to a young girl repulsed by anything with six legs and an exoskeleton.

A calf, after all, is a moist-eyed, warm-blooded creature that doesn't really frighten anyone, even though it's considerably larger and heavier than a person and could run you down if it wanted to. Besides, girls my own age ought to have been more horrified by the fact that in addition to innocent colonies of insects Hopevale also contained a death camp so efficient it made you shudder. Flayed and dismembered bodies were carted out of it constantly, ending up as bloody, lifeless lumps at the meat counter. Killing was what they did for a living at Hopevale. Murders and mutilation day after day! Cash registers ringing up death.

Death . . .

Bricks, my mind shouts. Bricks, damn it. I'm here to get a brick!

I march to the barn and start clambering up the rough-wood ladder. I raise my shoulders through the hatch into the dark loft.

My legs freeze, forget to move.

I see something that doesn't belong there.

Are the tears on my eyelashes bending the light in some odd way, creating a reflection, an illusion? I wipe my eyes on my sleeve with an almost angry motion, smell the intoxicating scent of the honey-soaked cloth.

But it's still there, as if it has always been there, as plain as day and as clear as the worn timber wall it opens out of.

I climb up the last few steps, and I can't believe what I'm seeing, even though it's just a metre in front of me.

HUMANIZATION

This is in response to the only comment on my previous post, an insightful and elegantly constructed argument contributed by commenter Blablabla.

It's often claimed that the human characteristics we perceive in animals are perhaps just our own way of anthropomorphizing animals (forgive me if this term is too long or fancy for the commenter). In other words, we see a reflection of ourselves in animals. We want to see human-like characteristics in animals because we're looking for reflections of ourselves.

It's true that there's nothing more comical than the trouser-wearing, cigar-smoking chimpanzees in old movies and film clips. A touching caricature that reminds us so much of ourselves, or is supposed to remind us of ourselves, and is funny for the very reason that it doesn't quite succeed.

But why do we have this obsession with humanizing animals and yet also have a need to obsessively deny animals' human-like qualities?

We think that animals are not sentient beings. Sure, they feel pain and hunger and maybe even sexual passion. But that last-mentioned trait is itself a touchy subject because it could lead to thoughts of love, and love is such an abstract, spiritual thing that an animal couldn't possibly feel it.

So let's start with love.

What about animals' love for their offspring, the way they care for, persuade and punish them? Mere preservation of the species, a function of involuntary instinct.

A pet's love for its master? A herd animal's nature, a reflexive submission to the alpha member of the pack.

The pair-bonding between two individual animals that looks in every way like love? Herd dynamics or maybe just a kind of automatic pheromonal recognition that their genes are compatible and will produce the optimal offspring.

But abstract, human-like love, *real* love? Heavens – no, sir! They're animals!

And yet anyone who has a pet is ready and willing to tell you how little Fluffy, Lady or Booboo has shown unmistakable grief, jealousy, longing, craftiness, guilt and premeditation.

But when it comes to farm animals these same signs of intelligence that we praise in our pets are just as rationally denied.

This idea of human superiority is just as blind, narrow and primitive as geocentric thought once was in astronomy. It would, perhaps, have been humiliating and degrading to admit that humanity was not at the centre of the universe, so when anyone proposed a sun-centred theory of the solar system they weren't listened to.

With the development of tools of observation it became apparent that the paths of the known planets didn't seem to conform to the assumption that they were revolving around the Earth. But everyone *wanted* the other celestial bodies to revolve around the Earth because the Earth was, after all, the centre of the universe, and that was that. So they attempted to explain these observations that seemed to refute the dominant concept of the universe, these anomalies, by developing more and more complicated hypotheses about planetary orbits. For some unfathomable reason, for instance, they created a loop in the celestial trajectory called the epicycle. A playful pirouette. Naturally, people were willing to believe this theory more than they did their own eyes. To change the trajectory of their ideas would have been too difficult.

When we take the many observed behaviours that suggest animal consciousness and emotional life and dismiss them as reflexes or mechanical instincts, attribute them to assorted on-off switches or automatic-impulse responses – a mother animal's cub dies; the cessation of nursing breaks off hormone response at an unusual phase, causing the mother to behave in a way that we might interpret as grief if we didn't already *know* that animals don't feel grief – we're invoking that same damn epicycle. It's at times like these that Occam's razor has its work cut out for it.

And not only do people anthropomorphize animals, it also works the other way around. I once read in a book about animal consciousness that dogs caninomorphize people. They assume that people behave like dogs. If a human comes too close to a dog that's growling over a juicy bone, the dog acts like it thinks the human is interested in stealing the bone, since a bone is a manifestly delicious, sought-after thing. Or a dog that's used to humans being above it in the hierarchy might show obedience and humility in typical dog fashion by urinating on the floor, which doesn't necessarily delight the human.

The commenter brought up pigs and cows. Do pigs and cows porsinomorphize and bovinomorphize people? Do they attach expectations and assumptions to us that are reflections of their own models of behaviour, and, if they do, what do we look like in their eyes?

Maybe they see us as über-pigs and über-cows, whose cruelties have to be accepted because right now that's how the universe is organized.

LEAVE A COMMENT (total comments: 1)

USER NAME: Seppo Kuusinen
You still haven't answered my question about where to draw the line with animal rights. Should animals be allowed to kill each other? Should a person try to prevent a fox from hunting rabbits? Is it all right to keep pets? Dogs, cats? What about dairy cows or bee-keeping? Should ducks be kept for their eggs? Should we eat shellfish? Can we kill an animal that is a threat to humans? A tiger, a wolf or a fly? A tick, a bacteria, a microbe? Furs are forbidden, but what about wool sweaters and leather shoes? Can we kill insects? Surely I can swat a mosquito if it sits down to feed on my arm?

DAY NINE

I take a step closer and feel a swaying in my head, my feet moving in small, wary steps now, like when you don't know if you're dreaming or awake or somewhere in between and you're waiting for your toes to touch the sheets or the blanket and reassure you that you're in bed, safely under the covers, and you can open your eyes and find some anchor in reality, some indication that your eyes have opened on to the familiar knotty boards in the ceiling, the paper lampshade, round and planet-like.

This must be a dream. All I have to do is open my eyes. I try to pry my eyelids open, but they won't open any more than they already are, wide open and staring, taking in something that shouldn't be there.

There's a landscape in the attic. The wall that should be a wall isn't a wall. It's a hole, an opening, and there's a landscape in it, like a picture.

It's as if I'm looking out of a window, except that I have to remind myself that the wall with the opening in it is an internal wall. Even if, for whatever reason, someone had sneaked in during the night and picked up an axe or a chainsaw and made an opening in the wall there is no landscape on the other side of this wall. It's not a wall to the outside.

I ought to be seeing the junk room through the wall, a dim space filled with junk, an old tin half full of window-frame paint, the pitchfork with no handle and the old kitchen stool, the bent fish-trap, the paint-splattered overalls hanging from a nail and a dozen bricks.

But instead of the room beyond the wall I see a rolling, sun-drenched, open meadow dotted with willow bushes, and far off at the edge of the woods a streak of blue sky above the moss-covered boulders. And flowers. A field of flowers. A dazzling riot of magenta, yellow and red among the green, almost too bright to look at.

The opening is roughly circular, perhaps a metre and a half across. It stretches from the edge of the sloped ceiling down to the floor. The doorway next to it that leads to the junk room is empty and dark.

I was just here. I came to fetch the overalls that I'm wearing from the nail on the other side of the wall not twenty minutes ago. But now everything's changed.

There's a window that isn't a window.

And if it were a window, there would be light falling on to the floor of the loft, the light would slant down and cast a puddle of light on the floor, revealing the grain of the wood, the edges of the floor-boards, but the hayloft is just as dark as it was when I climbed up. There's just this landscape, like a projected image. But it's three-dimensional and alive. I can see the wind rocking the stems of the flowers in the meadow, aspen leaves fluttering at the edge of the clearing.

I take another step, and there's nothing in my head. My brain can't process it. Although I'm standing right in front of the opening the light doesn't fall on me or on my feet or my bee suit, but when I stretch out my hand through the opening and into the landscape my hand and arm turn gold in the rays of sunlight, and I feel a gentle, warm wind like an enormous animal breathing somewhere far away.

I pull my hand back inside like I've touched a hot stove. It's so strange and yet so familiar at the same time, the feel of a sigh of wind on my skin here in this dusty grey building, this forgotten air.

I lift my hand again and touch the edge of the opening. I don't know where this sense of certainty comes from, but I'm absolutely sure that it hasn't been made with tools. My fingers feel the place where the beams are cut away. Up to a certain point it feels like wood, rough and fibrous, but then the edge of the opening changes to something so smooth that my sense of touch can't distinguish where the hole ends and the outer air begins.

I warily poke my head and shoulders out to the other side, and I can smell it – sun-warmed earth, the succulent aroma of the meadow, spruce pitch from the woods, the wind brushing my cheek with careless fingers.

I look down. I'm a few metres above the ground, about as high up as the hayloft is. Below me spreads high grass dotted with saplings and willows. A little further off are thickets of aspen and birch then dense spruce.

I push my upper body through the opening, all the while keeping the fingers of one hand hooked over the wall on the inside, anchored in the still darkness and reality of the loft. I bend over to look at the place where the other side of the wall should be, and I see – although the bright sunlight has momentarily dazzled my vision – the landscape continuing behind me, open and unobstructed, as if the upper half of my body craning out of the opening were half a person, floating in the air.

Nothing in the landscape that stretches in front of me and behind me looks like Hopevale. From where I'm standing, at this angle, I should be able to see my cottage on the rise a couple of hundred metres away, and further off the light-grey concrete complex of Hopevale Meats, but none of that is visible. There are trees everywhere.

I breathe in air so pure, so fragrant, so saturated with sap and moisture and so free of exhaust fumes that it doesn't feel real. And there's something else strange about it. My ears ache with silence. I don't hear the bellows of the bull calves at Hopevale or the rush of cars from the busy road a kilometre off. Just the rustle of the wind in aspen trees, snatches of birdsong and the faint, high-pitched hum of insects buzzing among the flowers.

Feeling light-headed I pull myself back into the dark, familiar, wood-scented hayloft and rub my fists into eyes, still stinging from the brightness. Immediately I hear all the encroaching sounds that belong there – the traffic on the road, the cattle and abattoir, a carpet of noise that I'm normally not even aware of because it's so familiar.

The opening is still there in front of me. It glows with the colours of late summer, the wind stirring its flora, yet I'm within four walls, under a roof, in a dusty room bounded by stacked and tightly packed logs.

I'm going mad.

This is post-traumatic stress. Hallucinations. Visual, auditory, olfactory, tactile hallucinations.

I forget about the bricks. I retreat to the trapdoor and descend the ladder. I wish I could turn my back on what I've seen, but there's only one way to go down a ladder, and, although I don't want to, I can still see the glow of the landscape through the non-existent opening for a moment longer before my head drops below the hayloft and my feet touch the bark and wood chips that cover the barn floor. There's a fragrance of drying firewood.

I glance up. Nothing but darkness through the hatch.

When I get to the house I take off my work shoes and bee suit, hang them up in the front room and get into the shower. I listen to the clicking of the boiler and turn the shower off while I'm soaping to conserve the hot water. I dry myself, take some clean underwear out of the drawer, put on my corduroy jeans and flannel shirt, walk to the cupboard and take out a bottle of whisky.

It just feels like the only right thing to do. I pour two fingers in a glass and look at it, turning the glass in my hand then toss the whisky down my throat with one quick gesture. It's just as nasty and burning as it should be, flowing down my throat like I'm disinfecting myself, right down to the kidneys.

I pour another shot and drink it.

The brain. It's an amazing machine.

What I saw must somehow have something to do with what happened nine days ago. I had just found the dead queen and watched the news. The world almond harvest had fallen by 80 per cent because of the disappearance of the bees in the USA.

So I was thinking about almonds. My mind was weaving together loose associations – almonds, Christmas pudding, Christmas – then

I saw the flash of blue lights from the direction of Hopevale, distant noises, shouts, and only then did I realize that a moment earlier I had heard something that I'd thought was on the audio track of the news broadcast. Sharps bangs: one, two, three . . .

That must be the reason for it. It must all be to do with Eero.

EERO THE ANIMAL'S BLOG
PONDERINGS ON OUR RELATIONSHIP WITH ANIMALS

TO ESTEEMED COMMENTER SEPPO KUUSINEN

You run into this hierarchical problem all the time in discussions of animal rights (as well as that most tired of arguments, whether or not plants shouldn't also be counted among sentient beings, of course).

It's true that many of the people who are ready to defend the right of mammals to live in a way appropriate to their species don't feel a similar empathy for birds or squid, although examples of both species' highly developed problem-solving abilities are well-documented. They just aren't one of *us.* Even a whale, which lives in a different element than we do, feels closer to *us* than a parrot or a magpie for many people.

But what about insects?

Is it all right to kill an insect? Or, rather, is it all right to poison those dreadful little plant-nibbling, disease-spreading creatures and stop them from disturbing our otherwise blissful lives?

I've never been able to fathom why the world is so insectophobic. It feels as if the common assumption is that if it weren't for insects (and arthropods like spiders, which many people mistakenly identify as insects) life would be more comfortable and less scary in every way. There would be no disease, no vermin, no armies of ants marching across the floor of the summer cabin. No *pests,* which nowadays refers to anything smaller than a squirrel. And the presence of these pests in humans' territory is a horror; mothers scream when they see something moving in the flour bag, fathers curse when they find a lively ecosystem in the walls of the sauna, and they grab a can of poison, even if the creature is a harmless silverfish crawling across the bathroom floor. Even an innocuous fruit fly is the trigger for a killing spree.

I've examined this reaction. For people today, when other forms of life come on to our turf uninvited it means losing the illusion of having control of our lives. A bedbug, for instance, lives on blood. It doesn't need dirty, unkempt habitations to reproduce, and yet, when a bedbug appears in a home, it's a very shameful thing.

I'm not particularly fond of the whine of mosquitoes on a summer's evening, but their existence happens to be inextricably linked to the fact that there is a bird singing in the tree. Every kind of insect is tirelessly toiling on our behalf, tilling and aerating the soil, aiding the decomposition of waste, cleaning the water we swim in.

And what about bees and other pollinating insects? It was the bees who 130 million years ago renewed the entire ecosphere when they provided flowering plants with a new way to guarantee reproduction. Even now there are about 20,000 species of plants that are dependent on bees. Cultivated bees, that is. If you include wild bees, there are 130,000 species of flowering plants that couldn't survive without them.

By the way, did you know that of all the genomically mapped insects bees are the ones that most resemble humans?

LEAVE A COMMENT (total comments: 1)

USER NAME: Seppo Kuusinen
Well, hell, bees must be mammals then at the very least. Right?

DAY NINE

I put the glass of whisky on the counter with a clunk. I go into the hallway and shove my feet into my plastic slip-ons. I grab the bee suit and put it under my arm to feel like I'm doing something real, something purposeful. I'll take it back to the junk room right now, right this minute. The new one's fixed with glue along the seam, and I'm sure it'll be dry and ready to use by tomorrow.

I march back to the barn for this supposedly important task, although I'm really going for quite another reason.

I'm going to get to the bottom of this. I want to know if I've gone mad.

I open the barn door and breathe deep and taste the whisky in my mouth. I already feel a slight pull under my temples. I look at the ladder and the dark open trapdoor in the ceiling. I climb warily up a couple of steps, the overalls hanging empty under my arm like a limp body, fragrant with honey. I toss it through the hatch on to the hayloft floor to free up my hands then go up myself, my head buzzing.

And when my upper body is through the door I'm greeted by familiar, dense, safe darkness.

Nothing else.

I climb up the last steps of the ladder and brush the bits of dirt from the ladder off the palms of my hands. I stand in the lightless, noiseless loft. The wall between the loft and the junk room is there, like any other wall, grey logs, the only break in it the familiar door to the next room, radiating dark.

I take a deep breath, filled with relief but also with a vague disappointment. For a moment I must have been struck by a baseless hope; if the illusion were still there then maybe all the rest of it was an illusion – the lights of the police cars, the banging noises . . .

But it was just a beautiful hallucination, an inexplicable creation of my unconscious mind, an unbidden attempt by one part of my brain to help another part, whatever lobe it is that's writhing under a pain that's almost unbearable.

Just to be sure I look into the junk room: there in the untouched, petrified stillness are the old supply of clay pots, the pitchfork with the missing handle and the bent fish-trap and the empty nail on the wall. The bricks are in the corner, peaceful and quiet, with the can of leftover white paint sitting on top of them, no doubt completely dried up by now.

I bend over and pick the overalls up from the floor, go to put them on the nail in the junk room. That's why I came up here, right?

When I get back to the house I have a third whisky, because if I don't I won't be able to bear the darkening evening.

I know that the human brain when it encounters a great crisis can develop all kinds of defence mechanisms. The brain can create perceptions that feel real, the feeling that everything's all right again, that the bad thing didn't really happen and you're not really buried under the ruins of an earthquake but safe at home, drinking fresh cold water. Or you can have hallucinations the purpose of which are simply to divert your thoughts from the source of your distress, to diminish the stress experienced by the body by redirecting your attention, if only for a moment, to something else, something wondrous and strange.

That night.

The noises. The flashes.

I don't even know why I took off at a run towards Hopevale Meats. Maybe it was a kind of intuition. An unconscious knowledge. Maybe a lot of little clues came together in my head all at once, things that I had seen, the meanings of which I hadn't yet perceived.

Or hadn't wanted to perceive.

I ran to my father's property, drawn to the flashing blue lights of the police cars like a moth to a flame.

THE INSECT WITHIN US

Our esteemed commenter Seppo Kuusinen was trying to make some kind of joke when he commented on my previous post that pretty soon we would be classifying bees as mammals. For his information, <u>Johannes Mehring</u> classified bees as vertebrates way back in the 19th century.

Huh? Insects as vertebrates?

That's right. Mehring felt that a bee colony is one creature, an organism comparable to the vertebrates. The various 'individuals' are parts of the body performing the functions of organs. After all, we don't give our pancreas or larynx the status of living beings. Although perhaps we do sometimes with the penis, from what the big boys tell me. :-)

But mere vertebrate status isn't enough once you really start to split hairs.

What group of animals has females who produce nourishment for their offspring while they're in a helpless state?

What group of animals offers their young a carefully designed and regulated environment, protected from the outside world, climate-controlled to a steady temperature of about 36 degrees Celsius until they're ready to go out into the world?

What group of animals uses survival strategies that include continuous, efficient learning and a highly developed system of com-munication?

In short, a bee colony, when examined according to biological criteria, is, in fact, a mammal. (The idea isn't my own. The first to say so may have been a man named <u>Jürgen Tautz</u>.)

A vertebrate. A mammal. But still much, much lower than humans, right?

Well, let's see. Bees are a species that has an advanced ability to control many variables in their environment and succeeding regardless of fluctuations in living conditions.

It's a species that produces its own food, stores it in a very efficient form and is thus able to survive for long periods no matter what happens in their environment.

A species that protects itself through defensive organization and closed, sheltered architectonic structures.

A species that regulates the temperature of its dwelling.

A species that is capable of forming concepts. Bees have been taught to react to symbols in mazes such as crosses and circles. A cross and a circle mean a turn to the right, while two identical marks mean a turn to the left. They'll go in the right direction even if the crosses and circles are replaced with other symbols or even colours.

A species that won't shit in its own nest. Bees wait all winter metaphorically crossing their legs and don't defecate until the spring, because shitting in their own nest would destroy the entire colony. This is something humans could do well to learn.

Apis sapiens, I would call them.

They are entirely comparable to humans in many ways, but the thing that distinguishes us from them is that bee colonies are, in principle, immortal.

LEAVE A COMMENT (total comments: 0)

DAY TEN

The new, mended bee suit looks good, like it never had anything wrong with it. I complain in my head about the way the world is: the most rational thing to do would have been to return an apparently defective suit, but since the damage was small and easily fixed I just didn't bother. Sending it in and waiting for a new one would have been too difficult and complicated. Right now, anyway. For me, anyway.

I would rather put it on and go out to the hives. For some reason I think of my bees as my real work even though they give me nothing but worry. My paying work is, well, paying work.

I went to business school like Ari wanted – it wasn't as if I had any consuming interests anyway if I couldn't make bee-keeping my profession. Ari counted on me becoming the managing director of Hopevale Meats after him. He would retire, go part-time and continue as chairman of the board.

It was like a movie. Of all the American movie clichés the biggest one, aside from the tart with a heart of gold, is the overbearing father, forcing his offspring into a mould, destroying a promising career as an artist – or some other endeavour the audience finds commendable – an evil force single-mindedly channelling his children into the pattern of his own values, a character whom the audience thirsts to kill, whether symbolically or actually.

Ari wasn't like that.

Ari had nothing but the best of intentions. Even when he went to America and left me in the care of my grandparents, thus pretty much abandoning his only son, it was the proud, simple gesture of a philanthropist. Ari was always striving to learn, searching for new models, training himself to think bigger and create a better future for me in the process. True, it was a model that turned out to benefit him as well, but he was thinking of me. He didn't want me to end up scraping by as a small farmer pottering around with my bees like Pupa. I ought to have cars, women, my own house and a couple of generations of pure-bred hounds.

I understand Ari's concern, his need to bequeath me an established, thriving business. But in the same way that Ari was planning what he thought of as a wise and correct course, I was, like all boys with any spine, having none of it. Hadn't Ari himself built an empire out of almost nothing? Gone off to another country, towards the unknown, to prove his initiative and ability to everyone? And what boy who craved his father's respect and acceptance would do what he was expecting me to do? No, respect has to be earned through what you do yourself, a solo race, not just humbly accepting the relay baton when it's passed to you.

Or maybe I just made my decision because as an adolescent I'd had no father to throw tantrums for, and now I did.

I have an uncle named Tero, born about ten years before my mother. After my mother died we didn't really have anything to do with that side of the family – we only kept in contact through Christmas cards.

Tero inherited a business from an uncle in another branch of the family, and he didn't want to run it. I don't know what made him think of me. Maybe Ari's business was so successful that it made Tero think we had some kind of genetic aptitude for running companies. When I read his email it made me smile, but I called him on the number he'd sent, and we arranged to meet.

He took me to where the business was, and I could see right away that there was something about the look of the place that worked. If there ever was a visual representation of the smell of death, they'd captured it.

The display windows were entirely covered in a black plastic film.

The dreariness of the rain-spattered shop front lit by slanting spring sunlight, the rain-streaked dirt on the large front window spoke the inexorable language of the way of all dust. The window said ARWIDSSON'S FUNERAL SERVICES in stick-on letters peeling at the edges. But the location wasn't bad, I sensed that almost automatically.

My uncle took a bundle of jangling keys out of his anorak pocket, and we stepped inside. Although it was a beautiful March day the blacked-out window meant we had to turn on all the lights. They came on with a fluttering sound, as if the dead flies that dotted the glass of the fluorescent tubes had suddenly been resurrected.

The gloomy front room of the shop was dominated by coffins on raised, bunkbed-like platforms. As my uncle walked past them I noticed that the breeze of his passing stirred the pale gold tassels that hung at the corners of each platform, sending motes of dust drifting into the air. The coffins were decorated with kitschy, cheap-looking crosses. Plywood peeped out from under the poorly made, yellowed drapery covering the platforms.

I caught myself thinking, I'd die before I'd be buried in a coffin like that.

Uncle Tero showed me the coffins then blew the dust off a red plastic folder that he took from a shelf on the wall.

'This is the stone catalogue.' He turned pages of floppy plastic pockets filled with what looked like snapshots of graves taken with a cheap camera, some blurred, all of them indifferently lit. Most of the stones were grim, upright, polished rectangles with two options for lettering – carved or gilded. Then there were a few deluxe models, basically curved-edged rectangles with a choice of two carved figures – an angel or praying hands.

'My uncle had a good contract with this stonecutter. You present these to the customer, sell them a little, get a good commission. When they're in that situation they don't usually want to start shopping and comparing prices.'

I tried to clear my thoughts and adapt my marketing education to this unaccustomed, somewhat macabre world.

This was an essential product and service. That was undeniable.

There would always be a place for it. The target market never changed. It wasn't a business that fluctuated with the trends. Or did it? I would just have to find out.

But how would you control demand? How would you develop your service? This wasn't a day-to-day product or an impulse purchase to make life a little easier. When it comes to food, it's a simple matter to develop time-saving convenience foods, ready-to-heat servings of pasta for people who can't wait ten minutes for water to boil, pre-cut frozen potatoes and onions for people who don't know which end of a knife to hold. Those things sold. But for a product like this you couldn't use some slogan like 'From morgue to mausoleum in less than six hours'.

Then it occurred to me: a negative need. Like toilet paper when there isn't any. The truisms don't apply. A situation that comes up totally unexpectedly, maybe for the first time. Something has changed in an unpleasant way, and it has to be taken care of, placed out of sight.

If the customer's condition is stripped of all its emotion, it's basically just like the demand that's created when you hit an elk with your car and you're shocked to the core and gratefully ready to pay someone to handle it, someone whose job is to clear animal carcasses off the highway and tow cars to the breaker's yard, someone who can tell you how the insurance works in these situations.

'It isn't rocket science,' my uncle says. 'You put on a suit, say the right things. The customers will usually tell you what they want. Whether they're hoping for an oak coffin – for some reason older men always want it made out of oak. Then you ask if the family has a burial plot and so on.'

Say the right things?

'You know, don't say die or death or body. Talk about the departed or passing into eternity or maybe just be simple and say the deceased. It's hard to avoid talking about it when you're arranging the transport, for instance, so deceased is a good choice. And then you sell the coffin and the headstone. Good commissions. You make a deal with a caterer, and you get something from that, too, since you're steering business their way. A customer in that situation doesn't necessarily want to think about what to put in the sandwiches or whether to serve shortbread with the coffee.'

I flipped through the pictures of headstones. What if I were a newly widowed wife who had significant liquidity collecting in a drawer somewhere and was faced with this *negative need*? In that situation wouldn't it be awful to be forced to buy something ugly just because I had no alternative? Once they've walked into a funeral director's would anyone dare to start quibbling about the headstone design or complaining that the deceased was a Japanophile so why couldn't they serve sushi at the wake?

I thought there must be people who, even in a time of negative need, would still only buy a certain kind of patterned and embossed toilet paper. It may be a negative need, but it's important to them that even if a thing is unavoidable you are paying for it after all, and it would be nice if it at least didn't look crappy.

Crappy. I just about managed to stifle a laugh. But wasn't it true, for heaven's sake? Wasn't it just the circle of life made visible at both the macro and micro level? There was dead matter that needed to be removed from the system. Sometimes you sent it on its way in shame and secrecy with a flush down the toilet, at other times you gave it a flyover and a 21-gun salute. In both cases you're talking about biomass removed from its connection to consciousness.

I realized that you could approach this thing with the same kind of premium pride that you had with any other unavoidable thing that we avoid in life. You could think about it in the same biologically neutral, antiseptic, coldly economic terms as toilet paper. Toilet paper could still be soft, pleasingly designed, beautifully packaged and expensive.

We aren't grim reapers ourselves, we're merely Charon's ferrymen.

We aren't surrounded by the stench of death. We aren't the police, doctors, firemen, ambulance crews or hospice workers. We don't dive into smoke, scorch ourselves in a sea of flames. We don't fight to the very last with defibrillators, shots of adrenaline or CPR. We don't stare at the EEG or ECG monitor with a desperate look in our eyes or sigh with desolation when all hope is lost. We're the ones you call when the truth has already come crashing down, when nothing can be done. We aren't to blame for anything.

Well, actually, that's not quite true. If something goes wrong in the ceremony, if the urn falls over and the casual summer staff pretend not to notice, if the Karelian pies on the coffee service dry out or the whipped cream turns yellow, if the photographer's hungover and doesn't get a record of all the mourners, then we're the ones they complain to, the shoulder that all the tears of frustration are cried on, along with the tears for the fact that Dad never paid any attention to Mum's drinking, that the aunt who just rolled into eternity in her wheelchair promised them the silver candlesticks, but their brother's sneaky son took them. You're there for them, a service professional, a person, a shoulder, and you hand them a moisturized tissue from the shelf in the reception room (those special Kleenexes that Salme recommended).

Salme. She was a chapter unto herself. She had professional experience, I don't deny that. But when I took charge of the business I changed all the rules.

I remodelled the shop from top to bottom, gave it soft light, almost like a living-room. A sofa set, silk cushions, modern Scandinavian furniture. Soft classical music playing in the background.

We're a full-service establishment. Our coffin, headstone and urn selection is unparalleled in quality and style. We even order items from abroad.

I thought about the name of the business for a long time. Eventually I got the idea from a headstone design referred to as the suitcase model. If the stone was the deceased person's suitcase, then we were their Port of Departure.

Salme no longer suited the style of Port of Departure. She was somewhere between forty and sixty – it hardly mattered. She dressed in pearl-grey blazers over a rotating selection of pale-blue and lavender-pink blouses, and she knew the stoneworks sales rep and the coffin wholesaler by their first names.

Salme was just the kind of pious 'Olga Golgatha' people might unconsciously want to meet when they went to a funeral director's. That was part of what made me want to get rid of her – her liturgical tone when speaking, the flood of euphemisms she used, just as Tero recommended, about 'passing' and going to a 'final resting place'. What's wrong with straightforward, neutral words such as body, death or grave?

Of course, you need to know how to honour grief, too, and not go overboard with overly casual language.

That's why Teemu was let go. Teemu was the hearse driver and handyman. His national service had been in non-military capacity – a lanky fellow with a bad complexion whose hair was always a bit untidy (although this was hardly anything to do with not having served in the military; he was just lazy). Teemu's problem was that he tried to be casual about death. He called the hearse the 'carcass cart', the burial the 'big dig' and the crematorium the 'grill'. 'Shall we toss this meat on the grill?' he might say, 'Pop these ashes in a jar?' In addition to jar, he sometimes called the urn the 'jug'; the coffin he referred to as the 'crate' and the flower arrangements as the 'veg'. He didn't talk that way in front of the customers, of course, but I would get a ringing in my ears when he came in for a coffee break and said, stony-faced, 'How many stiffs we putting in the dirt this week?'

I hired a well-built, quiet army veteran to replace him. I think being pleasant to look at is not at all a bad thing for a person working in a funeral director's. And I never would have guessed that a young man who'd been in the army would be so much better at the job than one who hadn't. Maybe it was his military training – but there was something paradoxical in that. A man trained as a dispenser of death had an unmistakably stronger respect for death.

Once Eero came with me to pick up a body from the hospital. He was four or five years old. He was curious and focused, as always. The human body we were putting in the coffin interested him just a little.

He asked why the man wasn't moving, and I told him that the man was dead. The word clearly interested him; he'd heard it so many times on television.

He followed up – although at that age he was considerably more interested in the tassels on the coffin and the mysterious-looking embroidery on the burial robe – by asking whether dying was like sleeping, and I said not really, because when you die you don't wake up. And every one of us will die when our time comes, but that usually doesn't happen until we're very, very old or very, very ill.

He asked the inevitable question, 'Why?'

I said that if people didn't eventually die there wouldn't be enough room in the world for new children.

That answer suited him fine – he was a child himself, and as a member of the children's party and thus clearly one of that organization's beneficiaries (at least for the time being) the idea seemed only natural and fitting.

A couple of years later, when I was picking him up from a weekend spent at Hopevale (I was busy with multiple funerals, and Reija, Salme's replacement, was off sick), I found him and Ari in a surprising place: the yards at Hopevale Meats. Ari nonchalantly mentioned 'showing Eero around'.

I took a deep breath and had a sudden sense of what Eero had just experienced.

The permeating, coppery smell of blood. The spattered tile walls, the rusty patina on the concrete floor, the vats full of slimy organs like grotesque deep-sea creatures. The whine of the bone saws. The carcasses on hooks, their chest cavities ripped open to the spine, moving past on an indifferent conveyor towards the door behind which began – noisily – the decisive, crashing, dismantling of the bodies.

I looked at Eero. There was a little tight line around his mouth that I had learned to recognize, and his eyes avoided mine. His hand was still in Ari's like a loose, forgotten tether.

He wanted to be a big boy, to be brave, worthy of the gift of his grandpa's attention, but he'd seen too much.

And he didn't know what words to use to talk to someone about it.

I know I looked just the same when I lost my innocence. I was looking for an atlas on Pupa's bookshelf, came across a book on the Second World War and opened it at random to the chapter on Auschwitz and Birkenau.

A few weeks after Eero's tour of Hopevale he and I were at a large supermarket.

The glass cases were stuffed with beef, pork, lamb. Elk, reindeer, antelope. Pile after red pile, great heaps of it, almost overflowing the meat counter, lavish mountains of meat as far as the eye could see with blood and defrosting fluids flowing out in puddles that meekly reflected their own final destruction. Boneless, bone in, chops, fillets, steaks and shanks, all on display.

Even in death they draw our eyes to them, enticingly, provocatively posed. The tempting, dark red of marbled, well-aged sirloin; the sensuous, lard-layered curve of ham set at just the right angle. Minced beef illumined in bordello-red. Even the meat that was a bit past its prime was swathed in orange marinade like make-up to hide its age.

Eero stopped in front of the display case.

'Pieces of dead animals.'

His voice was hard, almost defiant.

Before I could say anything a woman standing next to us, taking her white paper package from the meat-seller, turned towards us.

'Ugh. Don't say it like that.'

Eero looked at her with bright, innocent eyes.

'Why not?' he asked.

She didn't look at Eero, she looked at me.

'You might try teaching your child how to talk about food.'

Death is my profession. My approach to it is calm and composed. Just like Ari.

If you compare Ari's business with mine he would be the knife wielder off his meds, the drunk driver, the bacterial infection contracted in the hospital – the thing that sends my customers to me.

He's on the production side of death. I'm more like the capable chef who, once the job of killing is done, arranges the deceased as presentably as possible on the plate so it can be transferred aesthetically, with due respect for its ingredients, into the great circle of life, a delicacy for the grave's open mouth, a tasty tit-bit for the always-hungry maw of the crematorium.

I slam my rubber boots on to the floor. One slaps against the tile floor of the centrifuge room, the other falls toe first and bounces half a metre into the air, almost comically, coming back up at me so hard that I jump to get out of the way. I stare at the boots, innocent in all of this. If you'd just stop thinking about Ari . . . I try to tell myself almost politely. Remain calm and composed, like I always say you are. Put your boots on like a good boy and go out among your buzzing livestock who are also blameless, although they're at least alive unlike this inanimate rubber that you're glaring at, grinding your teeth.

I sit down on the bench, pick up the boots and pull them purposefully on like I'm going off to war.

WHAT IS VALUABLE?

William Longgood has said that we are at war with nature, even if we do use pretty euphemisms to describe that war, words like advancement, economic development, progress. And in a war, of course, there has to be a winner. Or to put it in economic terms, there are winnings – what we wrest out of our environment and distil into money.

When I was little the concept of money was strange to me. Like many children I thought that money came from a slot in a wall or from the internet, but how it got there was mysterious, something only adults understood. Naturally I had a right to ask the nearest adult for as much of it as I dared, usually without having to do anything to earn it.

Once, when my father refused to buy me some gadget of the moment, saying that he didn't have the money for it, I asked that crucial question: what is money exactly? Of course, I knew that certain printed pieces of paper, metal discs and plastic cards had mysterious properties that made it possible to obtain things from the shop. But what was the magic? Where did it come from? Who decided its value?

My father took me to his beehives.

He told me about honey.

He told me how honey was a concentration of the energy of the sun. Bees need food for themselves and their babies, and they also have to keep their nests warm in the winter. They use the energy that the sun gives, which is basically free – the sun shines even if the bees do nothing. But a bee can't live directly off the sun's energy. It has to gather nectar. Nectar is what honey is made from. And bees have to build a safe place to store the honey. All of this requires work. A whole lot of work. A kilogram of honey requires seven million separate visits to blossoms, and for that the bees have to fly as far as it takes to circle the Earth four times. The work of bees also helps flowering plants to reproduce, so the bees are, in a way, constantly creating more employment for their species.

Honey is a distillation of work. The diligent flying and nectar-gathering of bees is transformed into the golden-yellow substance that makes a secure life – and steady job – possible for them and their offspring. The members of the hive who don't gather nectar themselves but instead do other work such as building honeycombs or taking care of the larvae receive pay in the form of honey, which provides both food and warmth, in return for their work.

Money is also a distillation of work. In order to get money a person has to work. Money is humans' honey, even if you can't eat it and shouldn't use it directly to heat your house. Instead you can exchange it for the results of another person's work, like food production or electricity.

'Or sweets or toys,' I said. 'Right, like sweets and toys,' my father sighed.

What my father didn't say Longgood did (I believe my father pinched his description directly from Longgood's writing), that there's more true wealth in a kilogram of honey than in all the world's currencies combined.

It's real work, the proceeds of measurable toil. We humans, on the other hand, destroy nature's true riches to make money, to create the illusion of wealth, confusing symbol with substance.

LEAVE A COMMENT (total comments: 0)

DAY TEN

Bee-keeping always has its routines, things in which you can become absorbed; a contained, orderly world. It's not really necessary to visit the hives frequently, but I do. I'm like dear departed Pupa, telling his worries to the bees, feeling like a member of a flock or perhaps leader of a pack.

I pull the gloves on my hands. Where was I? The new frames. The hive I bumped into. Have to stabilize it with bricks.

I go to look at the hive, to see if one brick will be enough or if I'm going to need two – and for a moment I feel a twinge at the thought of having to go back to the junk room, but I stifle the feeling. I'm a grown man. Sensible.

I march briskly to the row of green boxes.

I shudder involuntarily.

The hive next to the one that needs fixing seems quiet. Too quiet.

Since I don't see any movement at the entrance I pull the lid off the box and lift out a frame to look at it. I take out another. A third. It's just as I feared: not a single full-grown worker bee. Just a few apathetic juveniles. Abandoned larvae.

A dead queen.

A flame of fear goes through me.

Another colony collapsed. This nest is abandoned. CCC. It has to be. It can't be anything else. All the signs are there.

Nevertheless, I make a hopeless attempt to find some other logical reason, some combination of factors to explain it. I bumped into the box next to this one. The brick under it was broken. Could some kind of mysterious panic have spread to the neighbouring hive? Could the whole thing have been caused by that?

No. It couldn't.
The whole thing began many years ago.

There were several first-hand accounts of Colony Collapse Disorder written by Dave Hackenberg in 2006. He'd gone out to his hives in Florida and lit his smoker and found to his surprise that the bees didn't come out of their nests. Hackenberg – who had been a leader in the American Bee-keeping Federation and was thus not some crackpot – opened the hive boxes, and the bees were simply gone. He crawled all around the hives and didn't find a single dead bee. The frames were full of honey. And for some chilling reason there was no sign of marauders in the hive, as there usually would be in cases of abandoned nests, no other bees, no honey-eating insects of any kind.

Hackenberg had brought four hundred healthy beehives from Pennsylvania to Florida in the autumn of 2006. Two weeks later he had only forty left.

'There was nobody home,' he said. 'It was like somebody came from outer space and swept them away.'

Now, here, nobody is home.

I have to report this. I may have to destroy all my hives to prevent the destruction from spreading. But how the hell could this happen here, to me? Although varroa mites have already been found everywhere I've kept their numbers in check with formic acid and thorough cleaning. There's a mobile-phone mast on the other side of the woods, but it's been there for years – why would it start to affect the bees now, especially since a connection between the missing bees and mobile phones has never been established? And I saw the hives just yesterday, alive and healthy and filled with bees. If they'd contracted some new exotic fungal infection it couldn't have destroyed a whole colony in a single day. With parasites or mites or viruses the hive goes through a slow gradual death.

And if it was a pesticide there would be dead bees by the shovelful around the hive entrance.

But, like Hackenberg's, my bees have simply gone, leaving behind a few half-grown individuals and the queen, plus their eggs and larvae, sentenced to death.

In the wake of Hackenberg's discovery news of other similar occurrences began to pour in. In January 2007 there were reports of the colony disappearance phenomenon in twenty-two states, and some bee-keepers had lost as many as 95 per cent of their hives.

By March 2008 there were thirty-six states in the USA in which colonies had been abandoned.

In Europe disappearances were reported in Poland, Greece, Italy, Portugal, Spain, Switzerland, Germany and Croatia.

I think feverishly.

Ari. Can Ari have started using something new for pest control in his fields – maybe neonicotinoids?

Ari has several hectares of clover, clover that my own bees make a lot of use of, but even though I think Ari's capable of practically anything I'm sure he wouldn't use expensive pesticides on his marginal fodder. I don't know a lot about farming, but using pesticides to protect your clover sounds idiotic. Giving clover to feed-lot animals isn't even cost-effective – soy, malt mash and other high-energy fodder fattens them up to slaughtering weight much faster. Ari's clover field is just a gimmick to make the company look idyllic and close to nature. All of the photographs on the Hopevale Meats website are taken with the beautiful field of red clover in the foreground. The Hopevale Meats logo is a clover blossom and a clover leaf. Ari told me that he feeds a couple of head a year on clover and sells the meat to restaurants. 'Certified Hopevale Clover-Fed Beef' it says on the menu.

No, Ari wouldn't spoil the reputation of his clover-fed beef with pesticides.

But if hive collapse is here then Ari will be in dire straits soon, too. The price of feed will probably skyrocket, and quickly. And there are already rumours that the US demand is bottomless for any kind of animal feed, even Finnish silage fodder. High freight charges are the only thing that's kept the price low up to this point.

I put the dead queen in a catcher clip and slip it in my pocket. I have to make a couple of phone calls right away. I curse myself for not investigating the larvae and queen from the missing colony I found before, but I had . . . other things to think about.

I hear a small noise behind me. Steps approaching.

I turn around and see two men in police uniforms.

DEAR READERS

It's time for action, not blather.

I want to thank all of my readers and participants in this discussion. I might still be dropping in here now and then for harmless philosophizing, but from now on you can find me in a completely different place on the net. I hope you will find me, if you care about the following issues:

Crushing the life out of 'surplus' male chicks / chicks smothered to death in plastic bags / chickens' beaks clipped with unsterilized instruments / chickens dying of starvation after botched beak clipping / crowding that doesn't allow chickens even to spread their wings / withholding of treatment for sick individuals in order to save money / dead or dying individuals left lying for days or weeks among the living / lung disease caused by urine-saturated air / osteoporosis caused by excessive egg production / feet injured by wire cage floors / dehorning of calves without anaesthesia / pig castration without anaesthesia or other medication / infections caused by skin rubbed bare against wire cage walls / failure to treat sick individuals / individuals dying of thirst, heat or cold on the way to slaughter / live dousing in boiling water / unsuccessful stunning before slaughter / hobbling of animals / nose rings / stalls that force animals to remain immobile / pigs kept pregnant for the entirety of their sexual maturity / baby animals separated from their mothers so that they can become pregnant again as soon as possible / animals fed growth-inducing blood plasma taken from abattoirs / pigs' tails trimmed due to lack of space / animals standing in their own faeces / cows lowing for their missing calves for several days.

And this is just the tip of the iceberg.

LEAVE A COMMENT (total comments: <u>2</u>)

USER NAME: Gnoth seauton

In my opinion the paradox in talking about animal rights is that the discourse on animal rights is based on so-called liberal political morality and social philosophy — the individual and his rights are the starting point for everything. Talk of animal rights, in other words, is based on an ideology that created the bourgeois way of life and capitalistic hegemony but was also the cause of the present-day exploitation, suffering and factory production of animals — seeing animals as nothing more than a commodity. Animal rights (or, more accurately, the lack thereof) are closely tied to the logic of the capitalist system. Thus it follows that if you really want animal rights taken care of you need to question the overriding economic and social structure. Mere immanent-capitalist post-political 'green' consumer politics isn't enough. What's the address of your new blog?

USER NAME: Eero

Not telling.

DAY TEN

The police stand a respectful distance away. I recognize one of them, the one who's waving. It's Rimpiläinen, the local Hopevale police chief – although I don't even know what his official title is; his actual station is around a hundred kilometres away, but Hopevale has been in his jurisdiction since they rationalized the police districts.

He was here when . . .

I nip the thought in the bud, grind it in my fist and try to see the funny side of the situation. Two burly policemen standing around shifting their feet, pretending to be relaxed, but I can see that they don't dare come any closer because quite a lot of feisty bees are buzzing around the hives. That tells me that most of my colonies seem to be perfectly lively, doing fine. But for how long?

Two hives lost in less than two weeks.

In the eyes of the policemen I no doubt look like an alien in my white bee suit with a veil over my head, and they're on guard, as if at any moment I might command my army of insects to attack them.

I know why they're here, of course. The criminal investigation is still ongoing.

I really don't feel up to this.

I start to walk heavily towards them, a pale white ghost with a black, veiled face.

Before they get started they ask if I ought to use the smoker. I correct them good-naturedly – the purpose of the smoker isn't to frighten the bees away from attacking people; it simulates the threat of fire and puts them in a state where a bee-keeper can handle and examine the frames without harming the bees. I add a little tartly that anybody would probably prefer to think about something else if somebody came and tore the roof off their house.

We sit on the garden furniture pretending to be relaxed. I don't ask them inside. As far as I'm concerned they can sit on the narrow wooden seats, shifting their weight from one arse cheek to the other, glancing doubtfully at the beehives every few seconds. I don't even offer to make some coffee. Why should I? They haven't done – aren't going to do – anything particularly nice for me.

But on the other hand, they're not blaming me for anything. I'm just an eyewitness.

And an interested party.

I don't see any reason to change my clothes, although I do show some mercy and take off the veiled hat. I balance on the edge of my seat and go over everything for what must be the sixth time. I was in the cottage, I heard the alarm, saw the police lights, ran over there.

Eero's group of friends particularly interests them. I tell them I don't know any more than I did before. Although we had a warm relationship, a normal father-and-son relationship, Eero didn't talk about his activities at all. Like any kid in his late teens he didn't go over everything he was doing in detail with his father. He behaved the way young people always do with their parents. We didn't have open, honest father-son conversations with detailed accounts of which bands he first heard in a friend's garage, what careless convenience-store cashier he bought beer from, what girl he met at a party and got down to her bra or all the way to her underwear.

'Did you know about his contacts with the Singers, sir?' One cop asks, throwing in the 'sir' just to be on the safe side. I tell him that Eero was an animal-rights activist, that's all I know about it. He participated in demonstrations and put up online petitions.

'Read his blogs; they're still on the web,' I tell Rimpiläinen, although it was the other cop who asked the question. They already have his phone and laptop. They can find the addresses and the rest of his network there. Friends and fellow enthusiasts.

'And enemies?'

I stiffen. Eero didn't have enemies. The whole terrible series of events was a product of unfortunate accidents, grotesque, blind fate, being in the wrong place at the wrong time. They only meant to warn him. That's what happened.

The policemen look at each other. That's not a good sign. Then they shake their heads. Very faintly. And one of them puts a hand up to his mouth, just for a brief moment.

An even worse sign.

Rimpiläinen starts to talk, mentions Eero's other blog, written under a pseudonym, updated through an anonymous server. They didn't know about it either until they got a tip-off after the incident.

I ask how they know that some blog on an anonymous server belonged to Eero.

'It seems pretty clear to us. Careless hints here and there in the text. We were also able to trace the connection to your son's computer.'

I wrinkle my brow and mutter that I don't know what that has to do with anything.

'The comments on his blog sometimes got very rough.'

'And if you don't mind my saying so, with a certain amount of provocation,' the other cop adds.

They can see from my expression that I didn't know anything about this. And, haltingly, they tell me more.

By the time they leave the evening has already grown dark.

I've been dragged back into the world again, a world I don't want to think about. And I've been given new things to think about, a thousand nagging, buzzing, stinging associations, among them the fact that I should have known, I should have *known*, for God's sake, and maybe in a way I did know, but it would have been just one more unpleasant truth.

Festering thoughts: the guy who called once and started to describe in detail what he was going to do to me as soon as he 'got his hands on me' (mostly extremely violent acts, but also enough sexual ones that I thought he was just some pervert) and when I managed to get a word in and say something like 'Have fun, wanker', he was embarrassed and stopped.

'Wrong number,' he said, as if he'd suddenly realized that he was talking to the wrong Mr Hopevale.

Or those camping trips that Eero had every now and then. 'We're going to be out in the woods for three nights, Dad. It'll be educational. We'll build fires, sleep in a lean-to, be one with the forest.' That's what he told me. And he refused to let me spend any money on silly things like a down sleeping-bag or portable gas stove. Supposedly wanted to camp the natural way with borrowed gear.

A hell of a thoughtful son not making me waste my money on provisions even though I was making money like a pirate. And that artificial thoughtfulness wasn't necessarily even about my bank account. It was probably about my carbon footprint.

Eero was never on any overnight camping trips at Kintulampi. He was up to something entirely different.

And I had sensed all this, of course, like any parent does. You smell something rotten, but you hope that time will take care of it if you put off interfering long enough.

Eero was . . .

Just say it. A terrorist. Putting an eco prefix on it won't justify anything.

I won't think about it, won't think about it, wipe it from my mind with an angry stroke of an invisible hand. Too early to go inside, too early to have a whisky, way too early for bed. I have to focus on something, find something for my body to do, otherwise a sickly sweet agony will rise from my stomach towards my consciousness like vomit.

The brick! The brick to go under the hive, that's what I was going to do before the police came, before I noticed that the other hive was empty. I have to put a brick there, and even if it's too late for that hive maybe the others will notice that I'm taking care of them, that I'm diligent, trying to help. Oh my dear, beautiful bees, don't let this be colony collapse!

I run and get a head-torch from the house just in case, since there's no electricity in the loft. I climb the ladder like the hounds are after me. I don't even turn on the torch, like it would take too much time, like I must get this done even though the attic is quite dark. I stumble into the junk room. I know where the bricks are. I lift the paint can from the top of the pile with half-fumbling hands and choose two bricks. They're soothingly heavy in my hands. I go into the outer room and don't even try to climb down the ladder with the bricks, instead dropping them through the trapdoor down into the barn. I know they won't break because there's a thick mat of chips, bark and other wood debris on the floor.

Something flashes at the edge of my vision as I turn to step through the hole and down the ladder. A little extra light, almost like a glimpse of one of those annoying motes you see on the membrane of your eye when your eyelids are closed.

I turn on the head-torch. I turn my head. The beam of light sweeps over the dusty loft, the cardboard boxes, grey timbers with the chinking peeping out between them, the ancient tools, the pitchfork again, the timbers. The whole aspect of the room is different. The torch is too glaring, too penetrating. It's no help.

I turn it off. I blink and try to let my eyes adjust to the darkness.

A star is twinkling. Flashing in that darkness.

From such a deep black, the deepest black I've ever seen.

That blackness is on the wall.

There's an opening in the wall.

Again.

I just didn't see it when I climbed up in the thick darkness.

Now my eyes are adjusting.

I go to the opening. It's both strange and familiar to me at the same time. I still don't believe in its existence, but I have to go to it.

And I think that if this is an illusion then why don't I see the same meadow and forest, warm and colourful, untouched, soothing, flooded with sunshine? Why did I not notice the hole until I saw a star twinkling in an otherwise impenetrable darkness? Is my brain that clever? Clever enough that my hallucinations obey the times of day, so that . . . over there, on the Other Side . . . it's also night? A night filled with stars.

I grab the log wall with one hand, as if the opening to the Other

Side were a hole in the ice, with flowing current under it, and the wall were the sturdy edge of the ice, and my tight grip were the only thing preventing me from being sucked under and freezing to death. But when I lean out into the Other Side I can't help but notice how oxygen-rich, how pure, how coolingly fragrant my personal illusion is.

Adrenalin surges through my veins, and I can't help stepping back, turning and lifting the ladder with both hands and dragging the bloody heavy thing up through the trapdoor, grunting and groaning. I stagger under its weight as I turn it in the cramped outer room, shove it out through the hole in the wall and let it fall with a lurch to the ground a couple of metres below. It touches the earth with a soft thud, although I might have imagined that it would be sucked away into nothingness, into the hallucinatory depths of pure imagination.

The top of the ladder is leaning against the edge of the opening. The steps lead down to a sort of netherworld. I take a breath, turn around and reach a foot out and on to the ladder. I climb down clumsily. I look up and feel dizzy. From here I can't see anything that the ladder is resting on, it just slants up into emptiness.

When my foot touches the ground I look around.

The ladder is in front of me, and all around me is fragrant night. There is no sign of buildings or people, but up above me, at the top of a ladder leaning on nothing, is the opening, an opening in the air, an opening into an even darker night, which I know is the dusty darkness of the hayloft, a vague spot hovering against the sky.

I fall involuntarily back two steps, because now I'm looking at the sky, and I have to gulp when I see it. No, not just gulp. From some-where in the deepest cavities of my mind, salt water wells up. My face is wet, and the hand that's holding on to the ladder, on to reality, shakes in spasms. Because above me I see something that I shouldn't be seeing.

The sky as God intended it.

This pitiful northern sky doesn't face the centre of the Milky Way like the sky in the southern hemisphere, but a branch of the galaxy does spread across it in a glittering band, deep, multicoloured, in a breathtaking mist like sugar crystals scattered on black velvet. The

Great Bear is so close that I could reach out and touch it. I can see the Pleiades as if my fingers were reading them in deep, deliberate braille.

I can't stop the tears, because this world has no lights from cities or habitations. I'm looking at a sky like I'm in the Finnish version of an ancient Neanderthal valley.

The silence is indescribable.

No – it's not completely silent.

I can hear, or can almost hear, things that I'm not ready to hear. I don't know what they are. Maybe just normal sounds of wild nature that I usually never hear, large animals perhaps, moving through the night, and I twitch with fear, my organs filling with adrenalin, and grab the ladder. I climb up like a squirrel, almost fall back into the hayloft. I turn, panting.

I expect the opening to be gone, silently closed up, my brain finally returned to normality after this repeated, achingly beautiful illusion. But the opening is there still, the door to the Other Side, a route to a place so untouched that it reaches out to touch you. And all around me and behind me, just slightly muffled by the walls, is the outer world; I can hear the neighbour's teenage son revving his new ATV somewhere on the forest road. But when I put my head out through the opening, no sound from my own familiar reality resonates on the Other Side. Absolute silence.

There's something familiar about this experience. It comes to me in a flash. Once I went running in a tracksuit made of rustling fabric. There was a shower, and I tugged the hood of the jacket over my head. The fabric rubbed against my ears with every step, its hissing, rustling sound echoing into my ears, annoying and irksome at first, but I soon got used to it and hardly noticed it any more. Then it stopped raining, and I pushed the hood down, and suddenly the whole landscape of sound around me grew clear, calm, quiet, as if I'd slipped out of a roaring waterfall into still water.

The silence of the Other Side is just as big and pure and dazzling compared with my own world. I want to climb down the ladder again and investigate the Other Side a bit more closely, but I hesitate. I'm sure that the strange sounds wouldn't startle me again, because I'm very curious and I trust that warm darkness somehow. But the opening could close off at any moment at the whim of some power over which I have no influence (just as I have no influence over my temperamental brain – if the opening is some kind of imaginary hallucination my mischievous brain might very well decide to trap me for all time outside of the world I know).

But even as I'm having that thought about the opening appearing and going up to the loft again to verify its non-existence after I first found it, something keeps niggling, like a hair in my eye.

There's something about both occasions that's the same.

PERFECTING THE HUMAN SPECIES
A BLOG ABOUT THE ANIMALIST REVOLUTIONARY ARMY AND ITS ACTIVITIES

Welcome to my blog. If your search engine has brought you here thinking that you'll find some information on eugenics or instructions for achieving racial purity you've been lusting after, I apologize deeply.

The name of this blog is a comment on how humans have tried to 'perfect' animals, foods and nature and in the process have cultivated the barbarity, lust for oppression, greed and other imperfections in themselves.

The phrase 'perfecting the human species' actually has its roots in Finnish philosopher J.V. Snellman's writings (bet you didn't expect that, you skinhead Finnish patriots with your lion pendants). Snellman saw the protection of animals as a way to improve humanity, human goodness and the advancement of empathy.

The purpose of this blog is to present the activities of the Animalist Revolutionary Army, or ARA, from the point of view of its grass roots, to create a forum for the discussion of animal rights and to activate those interested in issues related to animal rights.

LEAVE A COMMENT (total comments: 44)

USER NAME: Terrorism is no solution
    You pitiful clowns think you're helping animals
with this inflammatory garbage, but you're just
hurting the whole animal-rights cause. In the 90s
when we were about to get a ban on fur farming in
Finland it was the so-called fox girls who went and
freed animals from their cages and caused so much

bad will that every decision-maker in the negotiations was infected with it. These things should be accomplished through discussion. What use is it to anyone for animals used to domestication to suddenly be objects of fear and cause car accidents and who knows what? Minks released into the wild are simply destructive, eating grouse chicks and eggs.

MODERATOR: E.H.

Thanks for your opinion, which includes some facts, in itself a rare thing. It's quite true that in the 1990s SPAY and ALF as well as the Rights for Animals organization undertook some actions at fur farms and other places such as butcher's shops that caused an overreaction among fur producers. (Some regular readers of my blogs might remember the term 'fox girls'.) It's also true that there is a mink population living in Finland now that doesn't belong here, but through careless farming many minks had already escaped from captivity on their own before the freeings you speak of.

We in ARA, however, are fed up with negotiations. When we let politicians publicly state that the starting point for the animal-rights debate is that 'Animals have a right to be slaughtered in the way in which they are accustomed' do you think their position can be influenced through negotiations? How well I remember the statement Sirke Peltokorpi, a True Finn in parliament, gave ten years ago in *Me Naiset* magazine when they asked her to name Finland's worst environmental problem. 'Definitely the wolf. Why are we all fussing about melting ice sheets when we have something to worry about right here in Finland?' (MN 10/2007). I'm not an avid reader of women's magazines, but that statement made the rounds of the social media and with good reason.

If all we do is stare at our own navels and think about our own wallets and the whole debate presupposes keeping an outdated, unethical enterprise like the fur industry on artificial respiration then the debate has no purpose. When the US spent decades trying to create some kind of general, affordable healthcare system on the Scandinavian model one of the reasons for opposition was that it would put the staff of health-insurance companies out of a job. Is that ethical? Did people oppose the spread of computers when it put huge numbers of printers out of business? No, because computers made life easier and better. When ships started running on engines was anybody upset at the disappearance of the sail-making trade? Probably not very many people, because motorized water transport was a step forward. Crying over fur farms or factory egg production is about as smart as decrying the end of the slave trade because it would diminish the poor slave traders' standard of living. (I'm sure people did just that, but now it's considered an impossible position to take.) The question of animal rights is just as great, just as important, as the question of slavery was at one time. It's a question of the obscene exploitation of living, feeling creatures, of inhumane treatment and unbelievably cruel conditions in the name of maximizing profits. If hampering and sabotaging these indefensible ways of living is the only way to have an influence then that's what we'll do.

SHOW ALL <u>42</u> COMMENTS

DAY TEN

What was the difference between the first time I saw the Other Side, when it was daytime there, and the time I tried to go and look at it again and it wasn't there?

I'm thinking like a detective.

I'd been drinking whisky.

It's a tempting idea and not to be totally discounted. I could try again; take a nip of whisky and then go back to see if the opening has disappeared, but my reasoning seems off somehow. It would make much more sense, would be more charitable, to assume that a mirage like that would appear when I was under the influence of alcohol, not when I wasn't.

I was wearing different clothes. Jeans and a flannel shirt.

As I ponder this I shove my hands into the pockets of my bee suit.

In the right-hand pocket is the clip with something rustling and fragile inside it.

The queen bee.

Now I remember, and I tear my gaze away from the velvet night of the Other Side and towards the door into the junk room.

My old bee suit.

I was wearing it. On that day, that evening. I thought I was wearing it for the last time, because I knew that the new one had arrived.

But I couldn't go to get it from town until a week later, and I hadn't gone to the hives either. That whole time was like a fog to me.

And it was on that same day, the day I saw the first empty nest. I put the queen into the pocket of my old suit, clip and all, thinking I would send it in to be analysed. And then I forgot about it, of course. Anybody would have forgotten under those circumstances.

Yeah. And then I brought the suit to the junk room.

And if I hadn't torn the new suit I never would have got the old one out again, let alone put it on. But I did tear the new one, and I needed the old one again temporarily.

I was wearing it when I came to get a brick. The queen was in the pocket, and the opening was here.

When I came back in my jeans and flannel shirt, after I had the whisky, the opening was gone.

Now I have a queen in my pocket again. The queen from the empty hive. And the opening is here.

I look up at the hovering bit of starlit forest night in the junk-room wall, then squat down and lay the clip with the queen in it on the grey floor. I stand up.

Immediately it's more cramped and dark. No matter how I move my head, all I can see is wood, just a wall.

I crouch down again, carefully pick up the body of the queen and stand up, swaying, my eyes closed, because now I'm afraid either that I'll see the opening or that I won't, I'm not sure which.

I open my eyes and look straight out through the round frame at an untouched landscape tinted blue and black, and the twinkling starlight and tranquil night radiates from it.

I look at the queen lying in my palm.

The first time I looked out of the opening it was daytime. Beautiful, sunny.

And what was my foremost impression? The hypnotic, rich, joyful hum of swarms of nectar-gatherers over the meadow.

Now I remember very clearly something Pupa used to babble about (it was Ari who called it babbling, in that gently teasing way of his).

Although he was a modern bee-keeper Pupa could recite old Finnish spells and runes. How did that one go?

Honeybee, bird of the air
Fly away and see
Ever upwards to the skies
Up to the seventh heaven!

Or that other one:

From the Earth the bee rose swiftly, On his honeyed wings rose whirring,
And he soared on rapid pinions, On his little wings flew upward.
Swiftly past the moon he hurried, Past the borders of the sunlight,
Rose upon the Great Bear's shoulders, O'er the Seven Stars' backs rose
    upward,
Flew to the Creator's cellars, To the halls of the Almighty.

I need to find more information.

But before I do I have to rest, clear my head. It's been a long, long time since my body's had what it needs. Things like sleep. Oblivion.

Although it seems horrible to say goodbye to the opening (I still don't know if I'll ever see it again) I pull the ladder back up and lower it through the trapdoor into the barn. I stumble down the steps, checking twice to make sure the queen is safe in my pocket.

I go into the house and carefully lay the queen's body on the bureau. I put an upended coffee cup over it so that no draft will blow it away or toss it on the floor like trash. My mind conjures an image of a lost bird flying in through the window and snapping the queen up in its beak, crunching contentedly.

But I do have another queen, the one in the clip in the pocket of the old bee suit, in the junk room.

If the thing's even there. I didn't check. Why would I? I just have to believe.

*

I brush my teeth and go to bed. For the first time in many, many days my firm mattress and cool sheets work the way they're supposed to. I let forgetfulness gradually wind itself around me.

PERFECTING THE HUMAN SPECIES
A BLOG ABOUT THE ANIMALIST REVOLUTIONARY ARMY AND ITS ACTIVITIES

FAQ YOU!

Since readers of this blog seem to be asking the same questions again and again in their comments, I've decided to put together an FAQ section. You're welcome!

QUESTION: Who exactly are the Singers, and what does the name mean? You don't sell sewing-machines, do you?

ANSWER: Our group is an international animal rights organization. Its original, official name is the Army Pro Animal Liberty, or APAL. The Finnish branch of the organization had the idea to use the word animalist, the name used by the characters in George Orwell's classic novel *Animal Farm*, and thus took the name Animalist Revolutionary Army. But because the ideology of the ARA is largely based on *Animal Liberation,* the well-known work by Peter Singer, the Finnish organization is commonly referred to as the Singers in the media. So it's a name we've been given rather than one we've chosen.

QUESTION: So who exactly is Peter Singer, and what's his deal?

ANSWER: Peter Singer's Wikipedia information can be found here. His ideas can be summed up briefly thus: humans and other warm-blooded animals should be equal. They should be treated well and be allowed to live in a way that's normal for their species, and humans don't have a right to use other warm-blooded animals for food.

Animals whose products can be used without having to kill them (like wool-bearing sheep and milk cows) should be treated as ethically as possible. They should be allowed to procreate freely, to live in their own herds or other communities, should not be shut up indoors except when the climate demands it, and their bodies should only be used when one of them dies naturally or when something like illness requires euthanasia.

Some members of our organization also believe that animals – any animals – should never be used for food. The justification for this point of view can be found in <u>Jonathan Foer</u>'s excellent book *Eating Animals.*

QUESTION: But if we stop eating animals won't we be restricting our food supply to a ridiculous extent?

ANSWER: A person certainly doesn't need animal protein every day, and fish is just as good a source of animal protein as meat is. Legumes such as soy are also a source of very high-quality protein that people could eat directly instead of cycling it through a cow's organs. Ninety per cent of the world's soy harvest is used as cattle feed, and the raising of cattle accounts for a larger portion of global warming than transport does. Methane emissions from cattle significantly exacerbate climate change, and raising cattle wastes and pollutes huge quantities of fresh water. To raise one kilogram of meat requires tens of thousands of litres of water.

QUESTION: But animals are just animals, after all. Why should we care about them?

ANSWER: We believe that warm-blooded animals (and many other animals, such as octopuses) are thinking, feeling beings capable of suffering, often able to solve abstract problems. Some of them use language. Animals are, in short, conscious.

QUESTION: If I want to support ARA's activities can I sign an online petition or something?

ANSWER: The Animalist Revolutionary Army doesn't believe in petitions, press releases or demonstrations. Instead, you can participate with us in direct actions. We have two divisions: the Tangible and the Intangible.

The Intangible Division specializes in informational rather than physical activities. It uses various viral means and methods such as social media. The Intangible Division digs up the truth about the mistreatment of animals and spreads it around. It's kind of like an animal rights WikiLeaks. If you want to participate in uncovering unpleasant facts and statistics about eating meat, publishing exposés on the unhygienic conditions of meat production, the treatment of animals in abattoirs, the diseases and disorders of animals on factory farms, the grotesque aspects of sausage-making or the negative health effects of continued consumption of animal protein, you are very welcome to join the Intangible Division. Of course, we're also looking for positive material, such as true stories of domesticated animals' ability to communicate, their empathy and their real heroic acts. We're happiest when we manage to rake some muck on the activities of individual cattle producers, abattoirs or animal breeders. Members of the Intangible Division have, among other things, infiltrated farms and abattoirs and worked inside production facilities producing audio and video recordings as evidence. The information they've gathered has been instantaneously and visibly made public. We're also looking for capable nerds, because the media isn't always our friend. Last year this area of meat production tried to prevent the publication of the information we'd obtained in this company's newspaper by threatening that this retailer would withdraw its ads from the paper if what we'd found was published. The Intangible Division hacked into the newspaper's website and within a few hours had succeeded in anti-marketing two meat industry players such that following their hack one of the companies was facing bankruptcy and the other, one of Finland's largest food producers, is facing an expensive consumer legal action.

QUESTION: Got it. And what about the Tangible Division?

ANSWER: The Tangible Division practises direct action. It regularly liberates pigs, chickens and beef cattle. Its purpose is not just to let the animals loose in nature because they wouldn't thrive there. ARA simply wants to make life harder for meat producers. Once meat producers are forced to track down their pigs from neighbouring fields a few times some of them eventually hang up their gloves and go into the organic-pea business. :-) We also have other forms of direct action, which I won't discuss here for obvious reasons.

QUESTION: Isn't your liberation of animals a form of animal abuse?!

ANSWER: There's no denying that most liberated farm animals hunker down around the doors of their prisons. It's the only place they know, unfortunately, the only place that represents at least some kind of safety and regular sustenance.

LEAVE A COMMENT (total comments: 61)

USER NAME: Idiots

Not surprisingly your club hasn't thought this thing all the way through. Did you know that at this very moment the woods of Oedema are populated by a relatively lively herd of pigs? I'm not talking about wild boars; these are wild pigs descended from the ones you lot set free. Now that we're having mild winters they're able to survive winter in the wild, reproduce and spread. A person I know in Sipco told me that they see them around the compost heap all the time, bold as can be, digging up and destroying vegetable patches in their allotment gardens and otherwise behaving like pigs — if you'll pardon the expression! City rabbits are nothing compared with these swine, I tell you! If one of these lightweight hybrid cars collides with a full-grown pig on the local roads the car gets the worst of it. The pigs that have survived for a few generations have been selected to be bigger than heck and aggressive and they're not the cute pink piggies any more, they have stiff, greyish black hair growing on their backs. You should be ashamed!

USER NAME: ProGL guy

Sooner or later Ordnung Muss Sein, if you know what I mean. And it'll be Endlösung for you hippies.

USER NAME: aren't they cute

Here we go again. Pampered brats making life hard for the rest of us because they have nothing better to do. If it were up to me you'd all be forced to move to the woods and live on pine needles.

SHOW ALL 58 COMMENTS

DAY ELEVEN

I wake up and start searching.

I go to the console and look some things up. The links and references soon form an endless, wandering labyrinth where I dance, reconnoitre, turn in circles. I don't set any bookmarks, don't take notes. Who would I send them to?

It's enough that the labyrinth starts to form a pattern that makes my heart beat faster.

The traditional stories of many cultures agree that bees have always been associated with life, death and, above all, rebirth.

In any mythology where bees appear they're almost without exception tied to the Other Side. They're sometimes even deified. And it's not just local stories – the myth is universal.

I'm no longer surprised that in almost every folk culture bees move easily between worlds.

Virgil wrote that bees possess a divine intelligence.

The shared name for the Indian gods Vishnu, Krishna and Indra is Madhava, or the one born of nectar. (And the Finnish word for nectar, *mesi,* is one of the oldest in the language and has its roots as far back as the Sanskrit word for honey, *madhu,* an etymology common not only to Finnic languages but also the Greek and Anglo-Saxon world, where we find the word *mead* to refer to an intoxicating drink prepared from honey.)

One representation of Vishnu is a bee in a blue lotus flower – and the lotus is, coincidentally, an ancient symbol of life and rebirth.

For the ancient Germanic people, perfectly ordinary air was

swarming with the spirits of the dead. And they also called the air by the name *Bienenweg* – the bees' road.

As recently as the nineteenth century the Mordvins worshipped the god Nishki Pas, the protector of bees, who controlled the countless dwelling places of the dead in heaven.

The Mycenaeans built their graves in the form of beehives because bees symbolized immortality.

When the Christians fled to the catacombs to escape Roman persecution, they carved bee figures in the walls as a reminder of resurrection after death.

In the Middle Ages it was generally believed – and is still believed in some countries – that if bees are not told of their keeper's death they'll go to heaven to look for him. In the southern USA beehives are sometimes covered in black cloth after their keeper's death so that the bees won't leave.

Eero often went with me to take care of the bees. But did I tell the bees about his death? No.

And the bees left. My, what a coincidence.

In Greece it was believed that bees had a close connection with the spirits of the dead or even that the dead lived on in bees. The ravines and caves where bees lived were roads to the Other Side.

I almost laugh out loud when an all-too-familiar example comes up, one so obvious that I'd forgotten it: in the ancient Finnish *Kalevala*, Lemminkäinen's mother follows her son to the shores of the river Tuoni, finds him dead and summons a bee to bring him back to life.

And then.

The most grotesque coincidence possible.

The search takes me to a page that I just skim at first, indifferent, then electrified, then with my heart pounding wildly. There's only one thing it could be – Eero's other blog, the anonymous one.

Perfecting the Human Species.

The blog the police were talking about.

The words 'bee' and 'resurrection' led me to it. I quickly read the post. He's talking about colony collapse . . .

I can't read it now. Not now.

I bookmark the page then realize that the website won't necessarily be on the web much longer. It's quite possible that the Singers will take it down or that somebody else will remove it, someone who wants to delete their ramblings from the comment section after the fact, for instance. In fact, I ought to have thought about whether I should, as a family member, delete the blog Eero kept under his own name. Nothing is ever really gone from the net, but still . . . The police already got the user name and password from the web server. They've left it to me to decide what to do with it.

It's possible that the website I'm looking at has already been deleted from its original address. It could have been copied and deliberately disseminated to make it harder to manipulate or destroy.

I copy the entire contents of the website on to the console's hard drive.

I remember a story Ari told me. It was stupid, but at the time it made me shudder. One of his friends, back when he was in the USA, had gone to visit Canada and sent him a postcard from just across the border at Niagara Falls.

The man was in an accident on the way home and died. My father learned of his death from his family and work colleagues before he ever heard from him.

Then the postcard arrived.

'Greetings from the other side,' it said.

Eero's blog posts are greetings from the Other Side.

Maybe I'll read them a little at a time.

But not now. I don't want to read them now.

I rouse myself and go back to what I was meaning to do.

I know, I know, my sceptical friends, I keep repeating as I slurp boiling hot coffee, my hands dancing over the console remote, you sceptics who have an explanation for everything, as if you were there, in ancient Finland or Mycenaea or India: the withdrawal of the bees into their hives in winter and their awakening in the spring may have seemed miraculous, like a resurrection. But that doesn't explain everything.

Why, for instance, didn't the hedgehog, who hibernates in the winter just like the bees do, become part of a legend of messengers between worlds?

Because hedgehogs don't have wings, you'll say. It's the *flying*, a thing people can't do, that gives bees a magical aura . . .

Well then what about bats, winged mammals that also spend the winter as if dead, living in caves and hollows, ambassadors of the underworld? Why don't they move between worlds in myths? Why not butterflies or any other insect crawling out from under a rock in the spring?

The life of bees was more closely watched, you say triumphantly, because they were useful animals, prized producers of honey! They may have been the only creatures known to all of our forefathers that withdrew for the winter. That's why.

'But,' I say (out loud, even though there's no one in the cottage to hear me), 'bees don't even hibernate.' Anyone can look in a hive and see that the bees are completely awake in the wintertime; they've just formed their winter cluster, with the queen in the middle, and they're moving and producing heat using the energy from their store of honey.

Which came first, the symbol or the explanation for the symbol?

Humans have looked at the world, pried ever deeper into the secrets of the cosmos and come up with bold theories on the nature of time and space – how there are an untold number of possible worlds, all of them overlapping, or side by side, or twined around each other like snakes in winter. To people, these are just theories.

But not to bees.

I remember the discussion of Colony Collapse Disorder at a bee-keeping conference in the first decade of the 2000s. One grey-haired bee-keeper kept grinning sarcastically and rolling his eyes whenever any particular theory and its implications came up. But he wasn't participating in the discussion, and finally one of his younger colleagues lost his temper and said, 'Does this guy think that CCD isn't a serious problem?'

'I use the term PPB,' the old man said.

We all frowned.

'Piss-poor bee-keeping. Some people said that was the reason Hackenberg's bees went missing.'

He cleared his throat and said in a troubled tone, 'I just think that there's no point in muddying it up like it's some mystery. It's obvious to me. You put them in hot water and they fly the coop.'

A stunned silence mixed with dismissive murmurings ensued, but the old man continued, 'Think about it. America is where the collapse is at its most catastrophic. That's the place where the bees are treated really badly. They're shipped around like cattle, migrant workers, slaves. A single hive might travel five thousand miles a year in a rumbling truck. They're constantly finding themselves in unfamiliar territory, the hygiene of their homes minimally maintained, no interest taken in their health until there's a mass die-off. I went there once on a sort of excursion, and you should have seen the colour of some of the frames those Yanks were using. Black as could be. They hadn't been washed in living memory. And on top of that there's the environmental pathogens, poisons, radiation – which even if it doesn't kill them is bound to weaken them – and once they've lost their resistance all you need is a rainy summer or a harmless fungal infection or some random virus, and the hive's really vulnerable. And then there's the lack of fragrance. The flowers don't smell right any more, which has to be tough on the bees . . . '

'What?' somebody yelped.

'I read it in the paper somewhere. Some guy named Fuentes researched traffic exhaust and its effect on fragrance molecules at ground level. Smells are dispersing too quickly. They don't reach more than a couple of hundred metres from the flowers. Before air pollution a bee could smell a flower from a kilometre away or even further. There are these fragrance compounds, and nowadays they oxidize before they're supposed to. Think about how you would feel . . . '

He raised his shoulders and spread out his arms.

'You slave all summer growing provisions for winter to keep body and soul together. You've got a barn full of wheat, a cellar filled with stacks of plump, juicy roots, fruits and jams, a woodshed full of more split birch logs than you can count. And then one day as autumn's coming on some big hand just reaches in and grabs it all and replaces it with a pantry full of bark bread and a shed full of wet sticks, so you manage on that and just barely get by without dying of hunger and losing members of your family to frostbite, and you survive a tough, gruelling winter, and then spring comes and you start up the same backbreaking work because you don't know what else to do. I for one would get fed up with it before too long.'

'So where do you think they've gone?' somebody asked.

The old man smiled. 'I wish I knew.'

Underneath the craziness there was sense in his theories. Maybe they left because they'd simply had enough; they were fed up, so they threw in the towel, tossed the tongs in the well. And since they had no place else to go they opened a door to another world.

Our ancestors knew something about bees that we've forgotten or refuse to recognize, that bees, with their incomparable senses, can sense the thin spots between worlds and break through; use their efficient little jaws to nibble a hole from one universe to another.

SO NOW I WANNA GO AND LIVE IN THE WOODS?

In connection with my previous post I received a bunch of comments from the same person, or several very similar people, which can be summed up roughly thus:

'Just how are you alternative types going to survive in actual natural conditions once it takes more than a shopping trip to a pleasant super-market to stay alive and you're forced to give up your central heating? The only way to really test whether you have the guts and conviction for an alternative lifestyle is in the wild.'

This sort of argument is extremely common among opponents of animal rights. There are only two possible extremes: the life *they've* chosen – driving their SUVs to their oil-heated homes filled with the hum of all the newest electronic devices and tables creaking under loads of tenderloin, goose liver and Ecuadorian papaya – or the life *we're* suggesting, a life they picture stripped of all modern comforts, including supermarkets and central heating. Opponents of animal rights must assume that if they give our ideas an inch we'll end up on a slippery slope and we'll all be sliding straight into a life eating nothing but locally grown organic carrots, wearing itchy hemp clothes and living in a cabin in the woods heated by nothing but an open fire made of scavenged sticks. As if there were no choices in between that a person could achieve without really changing their standard of living: sacrificing a little consumption, enjoying meat in moderation, recycling, promoting renew-able energy.

I also don't understand this thing about 'proving you have the guts'. I don't know a single person who thinks life in 'natural conditions' is ideal or desirable or claims they could live on nothing but what they gathered in the wild. On the contrary, it's the meat-eaters who ought to be proving they've got what it takes. If they want to eat other animals they ought to have the guts to go to the woods and get the food for themselves instead of buying factory meat from a supermarket. People who recommend eating more plant-based foods are very aware of the fact that they're dependent on merchandise produced by other people. They just don't want other sentient beings to be killed for the sake of their consumer habits.

Reducing the amount of meat you eat isn't a return to some primitive 'golden age', it's an alternative for modern humans. We don't at all want to reject new technology – it's not like I'm posting this on birch bark, for heaven's sake – we want to use present-day tools to live in a more humane way. Modern food production is capable of feeding the human race without factory farming of animals.

Labelling us as opponents of progress is an expression of bad faith and a guilty conscience. It's a reflection of a lack of responsibility for the environment, an inability to change your life and your way of thinking, a self-inflicted blindness to your own cruelty. 'Nature is cruel,' you say. To that I answer with Jonathan Foer's words: 'Nature isn't cruel. And neither are the animals in nature that kill and occasionally even torture one another. Cruelty depends on an understanding of cruelty and the ability to choose against it. Or to choose to ignore it.'

LEAVE A COMMENT (total comments: <u>92</u>)

USER NAME: Lord give me strength

If we're really all going to give up eating farmed meat, what are we supposed to do, in concrete terms? Should all the pigs, cows and chickens be shot and buried in mass graves so the sight of them won't offend our sense of ethics? That would involve the extinction of many animal species. Do you want that on your conscience? You can't really set them free, although ARA irresponsibly does so. A cow that's well cared for has indoor heat, a chance to walk

around, a herd, unlimited food and veterinary treatment. What's a wild cow — an elk? Wouldn't you
defenders of the animals cry if somebody kept cows
in the conditions that elk live in? And what way
should a cow live that would be 'normal for its
species'? I maintain it's living in a well-tended
herd, being milked and then slaughtered. Every
animal dies at some point, me included.

USER NAME: JesseP
Have you seen the news lately? It may be that the
number of cows and pigs are going to decrease even
without our intervention.

SHOW ALL 90 COMMENTS

DAY ELEVEN

I climb up to the loft, resolute.

I've been to check on the overturned coffee cup. The dead queen is still there, sleeping the mysterious sleep of death. Let her be; I'm keeping her in reserve.

I fetch my old bee suit from the junk room, go into the outer room and put my hand in the pocket. I feel the clip with the other queen in it. It works immediately. At the exact moment that I touch the queen with my hand, just as if someone switched on a projector, there's the opening in the wall. Colourful and tremulous.

The queen lies on my palm, fragile, powerful.

Maybe the dead bee in my hand still has a lingering connection to her swarm, now gone from this world. Invisible, inaudible but as real as a wireless connection. A connection that opens a path for me, too, its accidental bearer.

Or is the queen dead only to my eyes, my senses? A friend with an interest in ants once told me that ants are basically blind and communicate through pheromones. Ants' nests have individuals who specialize in keeping the place clean, undertakers like myself, whose job is to convey their dead fellow ants out of the colony. A blind undertaker recognizes a dead body because at the moment of death ants exude something called butyric acid. Some cruel researchers rubbed the same substance on live ants, and the undertakers came and attempted to hustle them out of the anthill and on to the compost heap, kicking and screaming. Since an ant's life is dominated by smell, information from their other senses can be disregarded as relatively insignificant. I can picture the undertaker saying in an exasperated tone, 'Please stop your flailing, ma'am. You're dead.'

Our own senses might be just as misleading.

Every bee-keeper knows that even if hives are placed so close together that their entrances are separated by mere centimetres, a bee will unerringly return to its own hive. At close quarters this could be a matter of the unique smell of a bee's own nest, but you can move the entire hive kilometres away – as is often done in large-scale commercial pollination – and the bees will chart the new territory with lightning speed and return from a trip collecting nectar to their own group just as naturally, even though their entire environment is dramatically different from what it had been the day before.

Maybe they deliberately leave a queen in the empty nest that's left behind as a sort of anchor to which they can return if the new world they've chosen proves inhospitable.

I've put on a fleece jacket with pockets that can be zipped shut. I can't take the risk of losing the queen. I slip the clip into a pocket, making sure it's close against my skin through the fabric. It probably should be as close as possible, in a pocket, either on my skin or at most a millimetre from it, so that it's possible for me to see the passageway and use it.

I lift the ladder out of the trapdoor and lower it through the opening.

Sure and determined, I climb down on to the Other Side.

I'm not afraid. I have nothing to fear, not any more. And if this is an illusion, so be it. It's a good – in fact, a splendid – illusion.

When my feet touch the ground I start walking. The weather is beautiful, much brighter and sunnier than in the world I've just left. It's as if the place is untouched by the changed climate's inescapable and strangely damp winds, the tropically hot yet cloudy midsummers lying over the landscape like a sweaty palm previously unheard of in Finland. Here the wind is light, limpid. Everything around me is overlaid with the muffled, energetic hum of nectar-gatherers. The wind rouses itself for a moment, and I hear the tiny applause of aspen leaves.

I head off in the direction that in my world would be the way to the pond at Hopevale. Familiar and safe and painful. I'm interested in whether this world is topographically comparable to my own or altogether different.

The head-high grass and flourishing willow thickets are quite difficult to push through in places, but my body remembers the way.

The very first thing I sense is the unmistakable smell of water. After that I see it through the trees, a glimpse of watery blue. It must be Hopevale Lake or its equivalent here. It's only then that I make sense of what it is that's swaying in front of me, what the greenery is between me and the water.

The path to the lake is lined with a row of palm trees. Or two rows, to be precise. Date palms.

I must recognize them from some picture book I read long ago, their rusty red clusters of blossoms under an umbrella of leaves.

They form a majestic lane to the lake, as if some sheikh from a fairy-tale has come and planted them on an extravagant whim, here in the wintry latitudes.

An almost hysterical giggle escapes from my throat.

They're totally real, despite the ultra-Finnish landscape shimmering between their trunks, the willowherb growing around their roots. I'm overcome with the same off-kilter feeling I had the first time I saw a woman in a burka lining up at the supermarket. I'm not critical of immigration. I don't have particularly strong feelings about foreign ethnic groups or different religious restrictions on dress. It was just hard to fit the sight of it into my everyday circle of existence back then.

I wade through the willowherb along the avenue between the palm trees, and then something in the landscape stops me. It's a rather large boulder with a shelf-like protrusion jutting from it. There's a birch sapling growing from it that doesn't know that it's never going to grow large, that its roots are planted in a thin, grey layer of humus and under that is impenetrable stone and under the stone empty space.

I've seen that shelf of rock before, but it was much higher up.

When I was a child, it was as tall as my sun-tanned chest. Now it's somewhere around my groin.

It's not just that I've grown, not just one of those insurmountable obstacles from childhood become touchingly easy to step over. It's that I'm seeing the effect of the passage of time. And a lot of time has passed.

Pupa used to lift me up to sit on that spot on our way to Hopevale Lake. I continued the tradition with Eero. It was a resting spot, where we would relax a bit, take a break, and Eero was always just as excited to be up there as I had been when I was little, to be in a spot I couldn't get to on my own until my height started to stretch in puberty.

Now the shelf is lower, because the ground has built up over ages of fallen leaves and twigs, germinating plants that then decomposed, and the shelf of rock is where it would be after many, many years had passed . . .

Suddenly my memory speaks to me.

I was sitting on that tongue of rock on one of my walks with Pupa, and he had brought along dried dates for a snack. They were the kind that come in a flat, sticky slab wrapped in plastic, and we had cut it into pieces and were eating it, the sweetness of the dried fruit so piercing it made my teeth hurt. We gobbled them down, relishing their syrupy fibres. It was our shared sugar secret, sticking to our fingers, a reckless, manly camaraderie, and the hidden lumps in the middle, the stones that you struck your teeth on – always by surprise, it seemed – we spit out on either side of the path as we walked to the shore of the lake and back. And Pupa sang the Sillanpää March – *our marching steps are ringing out as one!* – and I with my mouth full of the sweet sugar of togetherness, singing, *our forefathers from a faraway soil are gazing at their sons!*

I brought Eero on the exact same walks.

We had dried dates, too, Eero and I. Those same little sticky, brown bricks with the treacherous stones hiding in the middle.

And now, from a faraway soil, these palm trees are gazing at their sower.

*

I walk along the lane of date palms towards the lake shore.

The shore is further away than I remember. The ground became higher, the shore turned to marsh and then dried up, or maybe something else has caused the shoreline to retreat.

Then I see something that is a confirmation.

Yes, this is Hopevale Lake. I can see the remains of the stone foundation of the boat shed, because I know what to look for – a lumpy, mossy, grass-covered, roughly rectangular bulge. The remains of the boats, if there are any, must be somewhere among these overgrown ruins. Nearby a group of pale-leaved trees is growing. At first I think they're silver willows because of the colour of the leaves, but the trunk is wrong, the crown of leaves a different shape.

And then I almost smile because, even though I'm taken by surprise again, I'm starting to learn.

Marja-Terttu used to complain constantly about the fact that the cottage, the former summer cabin and present home, wasn't on the lake shore. What kind of a summer cabin isn't next to the lake?! She wanted me to build a pavilion here, a good kilometre from the cabin, next to the boat shed, on a little spit of land that jutted out into the lake, to be a summer house for us. And it wasn't such a big thing to ask. I remember I enjoyed building it – it was just the right sized project for a cack-handed man like me. A four-square foundation then a few ready-made slabs of flooring from the hardware store and a tent canopy to put over it when summer came, with sides that rolled up. On summer weekends, if the weather was hot and clear, she liked to come here for picnic suppers. We would bring a salad and a bottle of wine in a cooler, kept a kettle grill in a corner of the boat shed with bags of briquettes and lighter fluid. And even though it was always her idea to come down to the shore (although I certainly enjoyed it, too) she always ended up complaining about the insects, and we never stayed for long once the sun had set.

Now I can see the barely discernible spot in the shade of the trees where the floor of the pavilion once stood. I wouldn't be able see even that if the materials hadn't been sturdy and weatherproofed.

Looking at the silver-leaved trees I remember with a shock what we used to eat here.

Marja-Terttu's favourite food.

Greek salad.

Tomatoes, cucumbers, plenty of raw onion and green peppers, with heaps of sour feta cheese crumbled over the top and a generous handful of black kalamata olives. Unpitted, of course.

Marja-Terttu would spit the stones on to her fork, and I less elegantly into my hand, but we would both lob them happily, slightly drunk on white wine, over our shoulders into the woods.

And now, here on the Other Side, in the ruins of the Hopevale boat shed, is a lush olive grove.

The certainty of it swells inside me, huge, incomprehensible and delightful.

This world has links to my own. I've been a part of what it is today, and so have Pupa and Eero. The bees may have chosen this world for their own reasons, but in a very tiny way it's my world, too. And Eero's. And Pupa's.

Our inheritance.

Maybe the 'now' of this place is a couple of hundred years on from my own time. The climate could be dramatically different, making this Mediterranean flora possible. Even without people, a climate can change. Or after people. Because there are no people here.

Because I have a bond with this world, perhaps even a sort of responsibility towards it.

And the fact that I found the opening on the same day that Eero . . .

It hits me again with all its weight, relentless.

I used to think grief was grey and spacious and insubstantial, like a damp fog that surrounds you on every side, one that you can't get away from because it colours the air, and you breathe it in and out, and it has its own earthy smell that seeps into your pores. I thought of grief as a fleeting thing like fog, like a damp that eventually disperses. One day the greyness is slightly lighter; after a few weeks the damp no longer collects on your skin, the musty smell diminishes, somewhere in the distance a pale sun flashes from between tatters of mist, and the grief dissolves into melancholy and then memory.

Never, not for a moment, did I think that grief could be as hard as a dagger, sharp and unrelenting. That it could strike again and again, always unexpected, hard, straight between my ribs, bright lights in my eyes, black and violet and pain so big that I gasp and stagger. I forget the dagger sometimes for a few moments, perhaps an hour, and that's the very worst – the stroke of the blade takes me by surprise, still just as hard, cruel, painful. It's worst at the moment of waking. I open my eyes, and for a moment the world is normal, the half-light of the room friendly, a new morning with a new beginning, the pure smell of unrealized possibilities – and then I remember. Eero. And the dagger strikes, has already struck and its serrated blade turns in the wound.

And the pain hasn't eased, hasn't diminished; the blade hasn't dulled.

The date palms rustle above me, their leaves sharp-edged and crackling.

There's another noise mixed in, low, purring, a much more familiar – in fact, beloved – sound, full of courage and power and strange hope.

Bees are working busily among the date blossoms.

I can still smile, a very little.

It's time to go. I've made my inspection, now I have things to do.

WHAT DOES COLONY COLLAPSE HAVE TO DO WITH EATING MEAT?

The disappearances of bees known as colony collapse increasingly reported in the United States – worrying and tragic as it is – has to some extent actually been helpful to ARA's efforts, since the dairy cows across the pond are traditionally fed alfalfa or clover. The cultivation of these crops has been seriously affected. Vast feed-growing fields have started to yield alarmingly slim harvests or no harvests at all. A few states are still able to produce the feed, but they almost certainly won't be able to meet demand. At first beef was being sold at a discount in America since so many ranches had to slaughter their animals because of the shortage of feed, especially soy. Now the shortage of both dairy products and meat has begun.

I've heard that to secure meat production they first tried feeding the cows corn, wheat, potatoes and rice – all species that don't require bees to pollinate them – but in spite of the uproar, the lobbying and the demonstrations, the US Senate was forced to interfere in the free market and sanction the use of grain and potatoes as animal feed, because if they hadn't the people simply wouldn't have had enough food for themselves.

The Yanks, who consider daily meat a right of citizenship, are, of course, demanding that the government do something so they won't have to change their eating habits. It is a sad paradox that vegetables have also suffered with the collapse of the bees. Although we in Finland have been spared from colony collapse, perhaps we should also start changing the wasteful habits we're accustomed to. Reducing the amount of red meat in our diet is beneficial both to the environment and the individual.

LEAVE A COMMENT (total comments: <u>159</u>)

USER NAME: Son of the North

I have northern genes. Finns didn't come here in search of refined carbohydrates — we came for fish, venison and seal meat. Our systems can't simply convert to vegetarianism.

USER NAME: Something must be done

Animals kill each other in nature. An animal doesn't distinguish whether its killer is a human or another animal. Other animals are often more cruel than humans, and they don't know anything about animal-cruelty laws. So should humans separate the predators and prey living in nature and lock them in zoos? What right do people have to allow the suffering in nature to continue?

MODERATOR: E.H.

Many visitors to this blog have already defended meat eating by saying that animals eat each other in nature and thus eating meat is entirely in keeping with the 'natural order'. Predators, however, have a carnivore's digestive system and couldn't change their way of life even if they wanted to. People, on the other hand, have an omnivore's teeth and digestive system. Early humans more than likely ate plants, grubs, birds' eggs and other gathered food, perhaps including fish. Large game was a rare indulgence. If humans had evolved to be carnivores they would have the intestines of a lion, the teeth of a baboon and the speed of a cheetah.

USER NAME: Defender of the cabbage

Why do you condone the killing of plants then? Is

respect for other species limited to vertebrates? If an organism doesn't happen to have a spinal cord, is it no longer a living entity to be respected, a mere bit of biomass to be cultivated and manipulated? If it doesn't happen to feel pain exactly the way that conscious creatures feel it should it lose all of its rights? Vegetarianism is murder, and condoning it is based on artificial, arbitrary habits of discrimination based on experience of pain, consciousness and taxonomy.

USER NAME: Logic
A carrot is a living entity, isn't it? What's next, a bean liberation movement? What does the savagely butchered fennel root have to say about it?

USER NAME: Tirsu
@ Defender of the cabbage and Logic, in answer to your question about the rights of plants: if you eat meat you 'kill' ten times as many plants indirectly. Animals are fed enough grain to feed humans countless times over.

USER NAME: Divix
Sorry if I'm being stupid, but why aren't they doing anything about the bee thing in America? Or is there nothing they can do?

SHOW ALL 152 COMMENTS

DAY TWELVE

I'm a good undertaker. Port of Departure is unquestionably the local leader in the field.

One of my basic insights about the funeral business was that much of what we do when a person dies is done to drown our guilt over the fact that we're still alive.

Primitive peoples' complex acts of appeasement of the dead and funeral rituals that lasted for days weren't just down to the fear that without them the dead would return to trouble the living. Because the dead return to trouble the living in any case.

I'm quite sure that every one of them is thinking, did I do everything necessary to prevent the death? Should I have done something differently? Could a decision made earlier have prevented the illness or the accident? Or if the person has died of nothing but old age they at least wonder whether they were good enough children, relatives, members of the community.

All the bustle surrounding the deceased and the posthumous praise are a relief to a grieving soul.

It is a paradox that respectable, full-service funeral arrangements rob loved ones of almost all of these beneficial activities. So, how can you offer mourners both things – a consoling, calming ritual as well as a maximum number of billable services?

The answers were almost too simple. It was a field that was extremely conservative, so there was an easy opening for a new track.

Port of Departure gave the survivors (and survivors is apt; family members are like wounded, stumbling creatures still struggling to make sense of their world) completely new ways to appease the deceased in as many different, personally appropriate ways as possible.

Take obituaries, for instance.

They're one of the services that a good funeral director's handles for its customers. The client tells you what the content should be – the mourners' names, for instance, and how long they want it to be – and the funeral director's conveys the material to the local newspaper. The paper then fits the announcement into its customary format.

I'd thought at one time that once home computers and easy-to-use graphics programs became more common personalized, self-designed obituaries would start appearing in the papers. There was no longer any need to choose from depressing, one-size-fits-all formats with their dreary crosses, always in the same font (a verse in italics, the family's names in bold), the only variations the approved insignia for veterans or the extra bar on an orthodox cross.

A lot of other changes had happened, too. There were a lot more people who weren't church members or didn't want a cross in the obituary for whatever reason. The papers offered these customers other standard symbols such as a ship sailing into the sunset. And then there were the members of non-Christian religions. Crescent moons or more exotic symbols were needed.

Some customers had the skill and desire to produce their own 'signature' obituary themselves, but that left a certain number of clients who wanted something different but didn't know how to make it themselves.

Port of Departure came to the rescue, like the cavalry.

I have Eero to thank for that. He was among the first internet natives, part of a generation for whom blogs, social media and everything else on the web was as unremarkable as books, newspapers, glue, scissors and correction fluid were to someone my age.

It was Eero who, when he was still practically knee-high, suggested that we move most of Port of Departure's services to the internet.

Soon our customer website had an unusually broad selection of excellent graphics complete with usage rights for vignette images. The assortment of traditional religious symbols alone numbered in the hundreds. There was faith, hope and love, there were a variety of angels from chubby, dreaming cherubs to rugged archangels brandishing swords. And plenty of secular symbols, too, of course – a bird escaping from a cage, a flock of migrating cranes, a swan, an old gnarled tree, a weeping willow. Flowers, from calla lilies to black roses. A mourning-cloak butterfly, a ripened ear of wheat, a sleeping child, a variety of candles, a broken vase, a flag at half mast, the River of Tuoni, Charon's raft, even a highly stylized Grim Reaper. Hobbies, subcultures, the image that the loved one clung to till the very last definitely had to be accommodated, too. I never would have guessed that one of the most popular symbols would be two crossed golf clubs.

In addition to the vignettes there had to be a good selection of quotes. Poems, aphorisms, verses. We collected hundreds and hundreds of them, carefully noting the original author of each. This was another area where we went outside the ordinary to find what was needed; in addition to traditional lyric poems and familiar phrases I listed lines from modern poetry, opera, Finnish and English-language rock lyrics and philosophers' musings on the futility of it all. I had quotes from Shakespeare, Schiller, Goethe, existentialist literature, favourite children's books (the Moomins, Winnie the Pooh, Astrid Lindgren) and bestsellers that dealt with love or disappearance. I didn't do all the research myself, of course; I paid a couple of literature and philosophy students to do it over the summer and got a wonderful collection of material for a few hundred euros. And whenever some individualist came up with some new quote we'd never heard, my industrious ferrets would add it to our collection. The families were welcome to create their own epitaphs, of course, which were, in all their homespun simplicity, sacred to us and thus never added to our collection.

I also ordered a variety of obituary layouts from our graphic artists. Customers could use their Port of Departure user name to sit in front of their own computer at home and combine images, fonts and words of wisdom like a jigsaw puzzle, and when they were satisfied with the result, save the obituary on our website for us to send to the newspaper.

Personalized obituaries sent by Port of Departure soon distinguished themselves as clearly superior. It was silly not to take advantage of that. I offered customers a reduction on the obituary pricing (easy to offer because the paper gave us a substantial volume discount) if they would allow us to put our insignia on the announcement. It meant that in the upper left-hand corner of the obituary it would read Port of Departure, in tiny lettering. Advertising agencies used to do the same thing in the 1980s, placing their logo on the most visible or creative newspaper advertisements, probably in the hope of winning a competition or to garner interest from those looking to hire an advertising firm. Naturally some of our clients balked at the idea and thought it was very tasteless, and I couldn't really blame them, but some of them were happy to get a discount, and a significant number, who overlapped with the former to a certain extent, thought the logo was a mark of quality, branding, a gesture that said that their loved one was led to their final rest with the highest level of professionalism.

Sometimes half of the obituaries in the Sunday edition would be signed by Port of Departure. It was marketing with a capital M. Once, just for fun, I counted the number of column inches of exposure for Port of Departure published in one month. I'd got the column equivalent of a couple of full-page advertisements in a section of the paper read very carefully by my principal target audience: the ageing.

With Eero's help and advice we made it so that you could also use the website to choose your coffin, headstone, urn or flower arrangement or to plan the menu for the memorial service or listen to suggested hymns and other music. I probably don't need to tell you that since Eero was helping me our suggested music included a lot more than the usual 'Nearer My God to Thee'. Céline Dion's 'My Heart Will Go On' was a long-time funeral hit, as was Sinatra's 'My Way' and Piaf's 'Je ne regrette rien'. Even Black Sabbath's 'Electric Funeral' was heard at many a heavy-metal memorial service.

But that was just the beginning. When I realized what a demand there was for personalized funeral services (we would drape the coffin in retro Marimekko fabric if the customer requested it) I also realized that even at this most extreme moment of equality – death – some people, or their loved ones, wanted to stand out from the crowd.

When I discreetly began offering my customers theme funerals it felt blasphemous at first, then logical and, after several decades, like the best idea I ever had. Why shouldn't the deceased's profession, beloved hobby or some other penchant be clearly on view at their last public appearance? The coffin, the decorations, the food, the music, even the way the mourners and invited guests dressed could be adapted to the theme. I've arranged a Wagner-themed Viking funeral for an opera singer, a medieval funeral for a history buff, a Star Trek funeral, a nautical funeral, an ice-hockey-themed funeral (with the deceased's ashes placed in an urn modelled on the Canada Cup), a Peter Pan funeral for a six-year-old (on his way to Never Never Land, where he would play for all eternity with the Lost Boys and never grow up).

It's as if I drifted into this business for the sake of this moment.

I know that many professionals would refuse. I'm not alone in that. A surgeon can refuse to operate on his own relatives, a priest doesn't necessarily want to ordain his own offspring, a judge isn't even allowed to preside over a case involving relatives. But I don't want anyone else to look after Eero.

The bullets hit him in the back. His face was uninjured. In the hospital there was a cloth wrapped around his face to close up his open mouth.

I've dressed him in the bright-red button-up shirt that he liked so much, the blue jeans with the knees almost worn through, the canvas shoes made of recycled fabric. No embroidered shroud for him.

He looks calm and serious. I've only added a little colour to his face. I don't want him to look cheerful and red-cheeked, like he's come straight from an act of protest.

The coffin is simple, the kind he would have wanted if he had chosen it for himself: natural wood, quick to decompose, non-polluting when it's burned. The shape is simple, like a packing crate.

Like a container to be cleverly loaded on Charon's ferry in tight stacks, an efficient, logistical use of space.

Eero's hands are on his chest. They lie one on top of the other, naturally, without any reference to prayer, because he would shy away from that. I thought for a long time about the flowers, then I knew what they should be. Nothing shipped from somewhere else, nothing grown in a hothouse prison, nothing exotic or wasteful. I picked a single sprig of thick-blossoming heather in the woods around Hopevale and placed it under his hands. The fluff of pale-pink blossoms, the dark green of the tiny leaves and the grey patina of the stem create a pleasant, eye-catching, almost harsh contrast against the bright red of the shirt. It's amazing how the shy purple of the heather doesn't disappear into the red of the shirt but bursts out, defiantly bright.

Eero was maybe four years old. At that age when he had a clear sense of his body and a large, extremely independent desire to use it.

Anyone who has a child knows how it feels to hold an unwilling four-year-old in your arms, how the slim little body suddenly stiffens in an arch like a strung bow when he doesn't want to put on his snow suit. How his narrow frame is full of will and slips out of your grasp as easily as a fish and, once free, runs so fast and changes direction so nimbly that an adult five times his size can't do anything but puff and grope for the spot where he was a moment ago.

Eero's energy was so great and irrepressible that I sometimes had to purposely tire him out before bath and bedtime.

'Shall we dance?'

'Yeah, Dad!'

So I marched in a circle, my hands under my arms to make wings, flapping my wings, bending and jumping, and Eero ran in his own wobbly circle behind, mimicking me.

Look, Dad. I'm dancing.

And I purposely kept repeating the motions, guiding him to the land of dreams, the honey sunset, the sweet, fragrant, blooming fields of sleep.

*

Before the coffin is closed and sent to the chapel cold room there's one more thing to do.

In my searches I found a folklore site that collected stories related to bees from different parts of the world. A couple of themes repeated again and again, regardless of where they came from.

There were dozens of variations on one of the stories. Two young men are walking in the countryside. They stop to rest in a meadow, in the shade of a tree. One falls asleep; the other lies dozing with his eyes half closed. The boy who's awake sees a bee fly into the open mouth of the one who's sleeping and tries, of course, to wake his friend up, but the friend doesn't respond, wrapped in a strangely deep sleep. Finally the companion is awakened, and at that moment the bee flies out from between the teeth of his yawning mouth. He isn't at all pleased to be woken up and says to his friend that he was having the most wonderful, utterly entrancing dream. He was wandering in a pristine paradise that he never wanted to leave, and waking him up had torn him away from it, preventing him from ever returning.

The older stories of untouched paradise were the ones most likely to have bees in them. Euripides – whom I'd never really heard of until I did this research – wrote in *Hippolytus* of an untouched meadow where shepherds didn't dare to pasture their flocks, where the earth had never been touched by the plough. In this meadow was a bee on the moist banks of a stream, but the flowers could only be plucked by one who was good by nature. Those who were evil didn't have permission to set foot there.

In the same play he wrote: 'Aphrodite's breath is felt on all that has life, and she floats in the air like a bee.'

I take a tiny, resealable bag – the kind they use to sell individual screws or a few buttons – out of my pack. My hive tool is in the pack, too. I hold the plastic bag open.

I take the tool in my right hand and with the other hand carefully open Eero's lips. I try not to startle at their coolness, although when I dressed him I shuddered at the lack of warmth. He has a slight overbite, so slight that there was never any reason to correct it, and it makes my task easier now. I put the hive tool under his front teeth and make a twisting motion – slowly, calmly, deliberately. Rigor mortis isn't stiffening his face like it did in the time right after death, and his chin gives way without resistance.

I leave the hive tool between his teeth to keep his mouth open. I pick up the plastic bag and carefully shake out the queen bee.

I put the queen in Eero's mouth.

I close the lid of the coffin and carefully put the plastic bag and the tool back in my bag.

OBSERVATIONS ON CCC, OR COLONY COLLAPSE

In his 2008 book *A Spring Without Bees* Michael Schacker asks whether the honeybee can be compared with the canary in the coal mine.

There were mysterious disappearances of honeybees well before herbicides or other by-products of modern life were even invented. The first case of unexplained colony abandonment was in 1869, and colony disappearances swept across the United States, Canada, Mexico and Australia in the nineteenth century. Before the modern term CCD (an abbreviation of Colony Collapse Disorder) the syndrome of hive or bee disappearance was known by other names such as 'disappearing disease', 'spring dwindle' or 'autumn collapse'.

But then it struck with a vengeance. In 2007 800,000 colonies were lost in the United States, and in 2008 a million. Some bee-keepers reported losses of 90 per cent of their hives. Although colony collapse was most noticeable in the United States it was certainly not confined to the USA. A great number of colonies were also lost in Canada, Asia, South America and various parts of Europe. In Croatia five million bees were lost in a period of forty-eight hours.

Of course, there have been theories as to the causes of Colony Collapse Disorder ever since the phenomenon first appeared. For a time there was a rumour spread in the world press that radiation from mobile-phone masts interfered with bees' navigation systems, but this was later written off as an exaggerated misinterpretation of the facts. The most fantastical speculation even posited that the bee disappearances were part of a devilish plot by al-Qaeda to cripple American agriculture.

One of the worst threats to beehives is the mite known as the varroa pheromonal destructor, which has spread virtually everywhere in the world. Australia was believed to be free of varroa mites until the inevitable spread reached its shores as well.

But the varroa mite doesn't explain everything. Long before it found a foothold in Australia in 2015 the continent was already experiencing a mysterious 'disappearing disease'. Colonies were disappearing now and then, just like they did in other places.

In addition to mites, fungus and other parasites and disease-causing organisms the health of bee colonies is affected by dozens of other factors. Bees are sensitive to agricultural chemicals. Certain fungi and viruses in combination with varroa mites can weaken a colony's vitality. And bees have fewer genes associated with resistance to diseases and toxic substances than other insects.

Colony collapse doesn't mean that you look at a hive and find the bees dead or weakened. The hives are mysteriously empty. This new phenomenon, CCC, or Colony Collapse Catastrophe, is more widespread, destructive and mysterious than any previous wave of bee disappearances.

At the beginning of the 2000s there didn't seem to be any interest in the United States in serious studies of the phenomenon like those already begun in France. The wave of bee disappearances had, in fact, prompted the French government to ban a popular herbicide. (Although it is interesting to note that colony collapse has also occurred in areas where they don't use agricultural chemicals at all.) No single cause for colony collapse was found in France either, but there is strong evidence that points to agricultural chemicals and their weakening of bees' immune systems.

So why was the subject studied in earnest in Europe and not brushed away? Simply because scientific research in Europe is not dependent on the support of large corporations. In the United States companies that sell pesticides, fertilizers and genetically modified plant varieties saw to it that colony collapse wasn't researched. It was a myth, a riddle – and it ought to stay that way.

There were similar attempts during those years to prove that climate change was a hoax; the intensity of the sun's rays fluctuate, ergo the temperature of the Earth will tend to fluctuate naturally over long periods of time, ergo climate change is not caused by people.

The key is to confuse, to create doubt.

To get back to smart phones, and their predecessor the ordinary mobile phone, there was a time when half the world believed that radiation from mobile-phone masts was to blame for the bee disappearances. I'm sure this belief was very welcome to makers of pesticides, fertilizers and GMOs.

Later that belief was overturned. (One might assume that phone manufacturers and service providers had a part in this. In a world poisoned by disinformation anything is possible, but it's more likely down to the rumour's origins in German studies of how bees behaved when cordless phones were placed in their hives. The electromagnetic radiation emanating from the device did disturb the bees, but the device in question wasn't a mobile phone. Since the article had the bylines of real scientists and the *Independent* published a long article based on this misconception the theory quickly spread around the world only to be discredited later.)

The horrifying thing about this rumour was that, in spite of the fact that half the people in the world believed it, *nothing was done about it.*

Bill McKibben has this to say about colony collapse: 'I don't think anyone really has a clue as to what's going on, but if it turns out to be cell phones, it's the greatest metaphor in the history of metaphors. Starving the planet in pursuit of one more text message with your broker seems the very epitome of going out with a whimper, not a bang.'

And what about genetic modification? GM corn has an added gene borrowed from the *Bacillus thuringiensus* bacteria that produces a protein that repels insects. It doesn't take a great stretch of logic to come up with the idea that such a protein might very well be harmful to bees, and in the United States 40 per cent of the corn grown is genetically modified. GM plant developers naturally strive to emphasize their harmlessness to the environment and may indeed believe it themselves, but history has shown that even the most thorough research can't predict every complication that occurs when you fiddle with nature. The infamous Thomas Midgley, Jr, who graced us with the creation of lead-additive gasoline, also invented freons. Mr Midgley gave assurances that the coolant was in every way harmless to humans and chemically non-reactive and demonstrated this by, among other things, publicly breathing freon gas. Neither he nor anyone else was able to predict that freon would damage the ozone in the upper atmosphere and would eventually be completely banned.

The only large corporation in the United States that showed any sign of concern about the effects of colony collapse was General Mills. Its daughter company, the well-known ice cream manufacturer Häagen Dazs, announced in 2008 that it was concerned about the disappearance of bees. Nearly half of the flavours of ice cream the company manufactured depended on bee-pollinated plants such as strawberries, pecans and bananas.

Michael Schacker, mentioned above, and many other authors have discussed colony collapse in their work. Every possible factor is suspected as its cause – the GM crops already mentioned, wireless mobile devices, agricultural chemicals, environmental stresses, pathogens, mites, viruses and combinations of any or all of these. One listener who called into a radio programme discussing colony collapse informed them that what was happening was a 'bee rapture'. The bees were being swept up into heaven because God had called them all to be taken up and to fly to him.

What's interesting is that no one seems to pay any attention to the fact that bee-keepers committed to using natural methods to care for their bees haven't really been reporting any abandoned hives. Natural growers leave more honey in the hives and bee pollen for winter feed – they don't replace it with corn syrup, sugar or soy. They don't use pesticides or other chemicals. Natural bee farms tend to be in the countryside where nectar can be gathered from wild flowers that haven't been treated with agricultural chemicals.

Unfortunately, natural bee-keeping is more complicated and demands more work than artificial methods.

It feels as if I've heard that before.

Fur-bearing animals. Farmed salmon. Chickens, pigs, cows.

Minimize the space; maximize production; skimp on feed and hygiene; limit to the best of your ability the animals' natural behaviours; respond to all the symptoms you yourself are causing with harsh, artificial treatments; use shortcuts wherever possible; don't worry about attrition, so long as you're profitable.

The shipping of beehives all over the country in the United States causes so much stress that the basic health and immune systems of the bees are weakened. Encounters between bee colonies coming from all around the country also increase viral infections, fungi such as nosema, mites and bacteria, which easily spread from one colony to another.

Selective breeding of bees for certain species characteristics (lower aggression, for example) may have produced a one-faceted genetic bottleneck that doesn't leave any room for adaptive mutations.

The corn syrup used as feed for bees in the winter is not at all comparable in its content of nutrients, trace elements and enzymes to the honey and bee pollen that bees themselves would enjoy in the winter if humans didn't plunder it.

In order to get the maximum possible pollination work out of a hive of bees, they are continuously, professionally and shamelessly deceived.

In the United States, for example, the hives are moved to a warmer climate so that the bees won't shift to their wintering behaviour but will instead continue working and reproducing. Sometimes the hives are given additional food because the more food a hive has at its disposal the more eggs the queen will lay, and when the colony's population grows more honey is produced to feed them. Some bee-keepers have reported that this interruption of their annual rhythm and artificially induced extra labour is driving queen bees to actual burn-out.

What takes the cake is that in California the almond-growers' association is paying scientists to do tests on beehives with artificial pheromones that trick the colony into believing that there are more larvae in the nest than there really are. That way the bees will haul in more nectar than ever and thus pollinate the trees with previously unheard-of effectiveness.

Am I the only one who hears this and is reminded of our work life nowadays?

Could it be that somewhere in the background we, too, are having a great hoax perpetrated on us, living against a fake backdrop, our nests doused with spurious pheromones so that we'll agree to work for someone else's benefit until we collapse?

There's another sense in which I've long pondered the way animals perceive us. Bees aren't necessarily able to fathom our existence. I'm sure they don't 'apianize' us, thinking of us as some other kind of bee. To bees, humans must be a malignant, tyrannical force of nature, a spiteful god who torments his servants like Yahweh did poor Job – paying faithfulness and obedience with evermore burdens piled on their backs. What amazes me is why the bees haven't risen in rebellion long ago.

LEAVE A COMMENT (total comments: 14)

USER NAME: Why always the USA?
  What I find interesting in this outpouring is its opposition to America. Surely there's all manner of mistreatment and skulduggery happening to animals anywhere you go. Why is it always the Yanks' fault?

SHOW ALL 13 COMMENTS

DAY TWELVE

When I get home the console monitor is staring at me from the wall with its taunting black eye. Twelve days ago it was a window into my son's life, an opening I could look through at his doings, opinions, sometimes with a warm feeling somewhere under my heart when I caught a reference to myself.

The console's eye is asking if I still want to keep my son inside it. Should I delete his official blog, the one under his own name, or perhaps make it a memorial page?

The Singers have probably already put up some sort of virtual monument to him.

I remember once in the early 2010s a loved one came into the shop and mentioned the shock he'd got when he learned a social network site was suggesting to people that they friend his sister, who had just died. I immediately took the bait.

Not long after that social media sites started to respond quickly to similar complaints, allowing families to cancel their loved ones' profiles or convert them into memorial pages without too much trouble.

Port of Departure was one of the first funeral director's to take on cleaning up the net – for a fee. Nothing can ever be completely removed from the web, of course, but you can delete home pages and cancel automatic feeds and maintenance programs. We also offered virtual testaments that could be created ahead of time, recorded confidentially and left unopened, in which the departed could list his or her internet activities, whether public or used under a pseudonym, and provide user names and passwords. Then when the person died their testament would be opened and our experts would delete or cancel the virtual life of the departed according to their wishes. Some people wanted to leave things like social network profiles to serve as memorials. In those cases the testament would include a 'final greeting' service, where the person, while they were still alive, could leave a message for those left behind, to be published on their profile or a separate virtual memorial grove after their death.

I was by no means the first to establish a memorial-page service, but the Port of Departure online-memorial-grove concept became the business standard for a long time.

Where others were satisfied to convert the profile of the deceased to a memorial page, Port of Departure created a separate memorial grove.

The memorial grove was a place where the deceased could gather materials ahead of time: pictures, video clips, musical selections, texts and links to pages related to the person's life or life's work. Some of the memorial groves were miniature Wikipedias, where even the smaller turning points of the person's life were thoroughly described. Although they may have never made the news in their lifetimes, in the end their memorial groves would tell their story, from the medal they won in a relay race in primary school to their high-school term papers to the only promotion they ever received.

After death the memorial grove can be public or restricted (through passwords supplied only to those authorized by the family, although sometimes the deceased doesn't let anyone touch it at all). Visitors can write their messages of grief, personal memories, greetings and eulogies on the page or link to audio-visual material. Most of all, they can light a virtual candle or bring virtual flowers (a wide variety, in very lovely arrangements available from our website).

Soon almost every obituary included a web address for a virtual memorial grove under the name of the deceased.

Port of Departure also offered a premium memorial-grove service that included site moderation. A person recovering from the death of a loved one doesn't necessarily want to sift through the trash heap of virtual graffiti left by enemies of the deceased or cranks that show up on any public website. Another service we offer, which has divided opinion, is Ouija. Loved ones still living who visit the memorial grove page can ask questions of or chat with the deceased. A simple word and phrase-recognition program searches the media profile left by the deceased and finds posts, comments or other activity to fit into 'answers' to their questions. Most visitors to Ouija experience it as true communication with the dead.

The Port of Departure memorial-grove concept is popular and extremely profitable. Before it was created there was no way to reconstruct a departed loved one from the shards of memory and give them a new life in the no-man's land of the internet for all eternity.

I'm not going to make a memorial grove for Eero.

It's three days until the funeral.

I go out to the hives.

Bees bustle at the hive entrances in the languid, late-evening light. The flowers are quietly closing in the shaded corners of the meadow, and the bees, too, are ready to call it a day.

I talk to the hives about this and that, like some people no doubt talk to their house plants. 'Aren't you looking lively!' or 'How's things over here?' or 'You need a little attention, don't you?'

I hear myself say everything's all right, there's no need to worry, I just wanted to let you know that my son Eero won't be coming to take care of you any more; he's gone away. Please pass the information on, and forgive me for not telling you sooner, but I've only just recently learned that such an announcement is customary.

The hive, the wooden box, is what I'm talking to, the animal I'm giving a friendly scratch with my words, a god I'm placating. Somewhere deep inside is its heart, or its womb, the queen, but its consciousness is divided among its buzzing cells.

Announcing the death of a bee-keeper might have very rational roots. In our ancestors' times hives might have suffered from neglect when their regular keeper was lost. Perhaps a new, competent bee-keeper couldn't be found right away, causing the colonies to react to the poor treatment by leaving and the disappearance of the bees was then associated with the death of the bee-keeper. The tradition of informing the bees might have even prevented colony collapse just because it served to remind people not to neglect the bees in their time of grief.

Our ancestors must have envied, and perhaps feared, the bees. Not because they could sting but because they were necessary and yet uncontrollable; they couldn't be tied in a stall, shut up in a barn or tethered to a post. You couldn't call them like a dog or treat them to a meaty bone or a drink of milk. And when our ancestors realized that bees had an ability to travel between worlds, a capacity to break through the walls of the universe when necessary to save the swarm or the species, they tried to use charms, magic spells and rituals to obtain a little piece of that divine ability.

Knowledge of this can be found in traditions everywhere once you know what to look for. It's been so watered down, so altered and obscured, that you can't always recognize it. But it's there.

In virtually every culture where honey is gathered it is considered a food of the gods and is also often thought to confer immortality. The bodies of great men have been interred in honey (this actually does prevent the body from decomposing, but there may be other reasons behind it as well).

In Wales it's believed that bees are the only animals that originate directly from paradise.

Porfirius wrote that the moon goddess Artemis sent peoples' spirits to Earth in the form of a bee, and – get this – after death the spirits returned to their own world like a bee to its hive.

I repeat the information I've gathered to myself again and again, hanging on to the sliver of hope it gives me.

And somehow, somehow, I'm absolutely sure of one thing – Pupa, who nailed the Hopevale beehives together out of discarded wood, put one nail too far from the end of that strip on that hive. A handle that years later would warp away from the side of the box and tear a hole in my new overalls. And it was a message, a purposeful act in the arc of space-time. It led me to what I've found. It was meant to happen.

PERFECTING THE HUMAN SPECIES
A BLOG ABOUT THE ANIMALIST REVOLUTIONARY ARMY
AND ITS ACTIVITIES

BEES AND AMERICA

In reference to comments received on my previous post, I don't blame the United States as a country for anything, and I don't have any particularly strong political opinions about it. It's simple history. Let's look at a few facts.

The European honeybee, *apis mellifera,* is an import to the American continent. When the first colonists came from Europe they brought fruit trees and other useful plants and seeds with them as well as bee colonies.

Without European honeybees the European plants wouldn't have survived, and as the imported plantings spread so did the bees. The original inhabitants of the continent soon realized that the European bees they'd seen meant there were newcomers in the vicinity. Seeing the European bees was a fateful omen of the destruction of Native Americans' way of life. They called the bees the white men's flies.

North America had its own pollinating insects, of course, including wild bees, but the Europeans' imported honey-producing bees displaced the local species from farmland and monoculture farming took care of the rest – there simply wasn't any corner left for wild bees to nest among the fields of corn, alfalfa and almond trees that stretched for miles.

Monoculture farming is the enemy of bees in other ways as well. Gathering nectar from a single species of plant doesn't provide the same dietary variation, nutrition and balance as buzzing through meadows of wild flowers. They simply become as malnourished as a person who eats just one food. Oatmeal is a healthy food, but it's not enough by itself.

And now that the Europeans have increased and filled their new country, harnessed its natural resources and drained and stripped great swathes of land, virtually obliterating the original inhabitants, the white man's fly has turned against its masters and left them up to their armpits in shit.

Nobody asked them if they wanted to come.

LEAVE A COMMENT (total comments: 62)

USER NAME: Masters of doublespeak

This ARA propaganda never fails to amuse me. First you preach vegetarianism and in the next sentence you yourselves admit that a person can't live on oatmeal. You make people feel guilty for perfectly normal enterprises like gardening. What are you vegetarians going to eat if there's no agriculture?

There is no doubt a natural explanation for the wild fluctuations in bee populations. There is, for instance, a variety of mole with populations that explode at regular intervals without any help from people. But you probably aren't interested in protecting moles; you'd rather jump right in and fuss over some even smaller critter. What're you going to start whining about next, amoebas?

MODERATOR: E.H.

ARA focuses on animal rights, especially the status of farm animals. 'Animal protection' is a dated concept that projects humans to a higher level than other animals, to guard and care for them. History has shown that what animals most need protection from is people themselves.

There are enough holes in your logic that I won't take the time to go over each one but will just state that when talking about the treatment of domesticated animals their size is irrelevant. What matters is whether they are allowed to behave in species-appropriate ways, and, if they aren't, what are the consequences?

The honeybee genome was mapped in 2006.

It was learned that bees have an unusually high number of genes associated with learning. But the gene map also revealed genetic weaknesses such as the fact that bees have a low number of genes associated with immunity and the elimination of toxins and are thus more susceptible than many other insects to various poisons and pathogens.

This has been known since 2006.

For a much longer time it has been known that bees are vital to the entire ecosystem.

The bees are starting to disappear.

Could there be a connection between these things, and should something be done?

Hello? Can anybody hear me?

From 2006 to 2008 worldwide Colony Collapse Disorder was the worst mass disappearance of bees in recorded history.

In 2008 it was predicted that if the collapse of bee colonies didn't slow there would be no bees left in North America by 2035.

Some joker made up a name for it: the Beepocalypse.

In this, as in so many things, the world is well ahead of our predictions.

USER NAME: Proggles not hippies

In the US they know that you Singers are behind this bee thing, so you can quit pretending. Your terrorists are poisoning and irradiating beehives. And you got the feed production, and through it the meat production, to collapse. Are you happy now?

MODERATOR: E.H.

You've got it all wrong. We're actually using our

vast spiritual powers to hypnotize the bees into
killing themselves.

And yes I am very happy now, because we've started
a real black market in meat in the United States.
You can always find someone who'll feed corn and
potatoes to cows illegally. And as far as we're concerned it can only be a good thing that Brazil and
Argentina are cutting down more and more rainforest
for grazing cattle. We've also hypnotized many
Americans into believing that we're behind all these
things, and even some bee-keepers who've lost their
livelihoods are blaming us. Thanks for pointing it
out so thoughtfully and accurately.

USER NAME: Tirsu
Oh no! You've caught us red-handed with our electromagnetic satanic machine built by mad scientists.

USER NAME: No user name
thanks for the confession the next time i see you
in a dark alley your fat arse will be black and blue
right quick. ps. i know where you live.

USER NAME: What's your beef
People have always eaten meat, and they always will.
Meat is nutritious and essential to the body. And
besides, it tastes good. That's just a fact, and you
can't escape it no matter how you twist your words
around. In a word, animal rights agitators would
prohibit people from satisfying their basic needs.
It's just as clueless and weird as prohibiting sex
for Catholic priests. We know very well how that
idiotic prohibition has turned out.

SHOW ALL <u>56</u> COMMENTS

DAY THIRTEEN

In the morning doubt hits me like a knockout punch. I squirm beneath it like I'm held under its thumb.

The feeling is familiar from childhood: the expectation of inevitable disappointment. I think I've done well on a test, then on the morning the tests are going to be returned my stomach sinks like a stone with the certainty that I actually didn't know any of the answers. In my mind I'm sure that the package that Ari sent, just arrived from the USA for Christmas, waiting to be opened, is a camera, but the next day doubt seizes me, and I'm certain that the package contains some stupid American toy intended for someone years younger than me, some remote-control car or toy tank painted in precise detail.

That feeling is back.

I imagined it all.

I don't want to spend another minute telling myself how real it all seemed, don't want to think about whether a delusion is less delusional if you doubt its truth.

Then one of the memories of disappointment steps to the front of the line, says hello and makes itself known. After a moment I nod. I understand.

There was no camera in that package from Ari.

Now I have two. There's one in my phone, of course, but I also have a high-quality pocket digital camera.

I wonder if you can photograph an illusion? If the queen opened up such a concrete passageway that I'm able to go through it, couldn't it also be recorded on a memory card? That way I would have some evidence, for myself, at least, to certify my sanity.

*

I climb up to the loft with the camera. I've put together a little bag for the queen and have it on a string around my neck, under my shirt. That way I can be sure it's touching me, and I would not drop it or damage it by keeping it in my pocket. With the queen against my chest I see the opening as soon as I come up over the floor of the loft.

The best angle for a photograph is from a spot just to the right of the trapdoor. The round opening ought to fit nicely into the frame. I decide to underexpose it a little so that the landscape isn't completely washed out. I lift the camera and aim at the scene and the hole around it.

When I look at the camera's display, there's nothing there but a log wall.

I go closer, right to the edge of the opening. I look at the display.

The log wall almost hits me in the face.

I look up from the display and the opening shines with the magic light of August, aspen leaves trembling in the wind, the glow of grass turning gold.

Drab, grey wood in the display.

The disappointment is so crushing that I fall to my knees and then sit on the dusty floor. The camera clatters from my grasp and lies on its side. I put my head in my hands, my elbows on my knees.

After a moment of deep stillness I realize something.

This isn't the first time this has happened.

When I found the opening the second time it was night. I could see the light of a star. But when I aimed the head-torch at the wall I couldn't see the opening.

I've buried that strange fact under all the other weirdness and wonder without stopping to think about it. Switching from bright light to artificial light in the darkness can play tricks on your eyes, after all.

Artificial light. Of course.

I look at the trapdoor and think about this whole building, as old as the cottage but left in its original condition much more than the cottage had been. It doesn't even have artificial light – not even in the sauna. I take my saunas with a hurricane lantern.

The California almond groves. Just yesterday on the news they were saying that they've trucked in new hives to replace the empty ones. The new hives have been fitted with every possible means to prevent swarming, and they're trying to monitor them day and night in person and with cameras. There's no way to tell the bees to stay, not to move from this place, but at least this way they can get some information.

And all they've learned is one thing: the new hives are emptying at almost the same speed as the old ones did.

Bees have been fitted with infinitesimally small telemetric trackers weighing just a few thousandths of a gram. But in some ironic twist of fate the bees with the trackers are faithfully returning to the nest. Just those bees, and not the others. All the rest have vanished into thin air.

The interviewer asked whether it wouldn't work to attach trackers to every bee in the hive and get them all to come back to the nest that way. The bee researcher could hardly keep the sarcasm back as he explained that, first of all, the trackers are very expensive high-tech devices and each hive has more than sixty thousand bees in it, and, second, every bee with a tracker that returned to the collapsing colony was dead within twenty-four hours.

Interesting.

Extremely interesting.

PERFECTING THE HUMAN SPECIES
A BLOG ABOUT THE ANIMALIST REVOLUTIONARY ARMY
AND ITS ACTIVITIES

TO OUR ESTEEMED COMMENTER WHAT'S YOUR BEEF AND HIS MINIONS!

We all have basic needs. This is true.

That's about the only thing in your comment that makes any sense.

The most important human needs are air, water, food, sleep and shelter. Without these things a person will die.

People have eaten meat for millennia. That is true. But there are also cultures of millions of people who have eaten nothing but plants and have indeed managed to survive up until the present day to tell of it. Imagine that! And I happen to know that there are many vegetarian foods that taste pretty good, almost as good as meat! The thought of this amazing paradox almost knocks your brain off its hinges, doesn't it, Mr. Beef?

To be more precise, there's a difference between *wants* and *needs*.

It's interesting, in fact telling, that in your discussion of denial of basic needs you mention sex.

Sex is a basic need of our species, of course, in the sense that if we don't have sex we won't reproduce and the species will die. But at the individual level – the level most central to our desires – sex is not a basic need. An individual will not die even if he spends his entire life without having sex at all, not even solo. (It wouldn't be a pleasant life but a life nevertheless. And there are asexual people who do just fine without it.)

Since going without sex is undoubtedly a way of life that would be unpleasant to many of us, some have designated sex as a kind of human right. For instance people who, for one reason or another, haven't managed to form relationships where sex is on offer should somehow have their needs met. Having sex with another human individual is consistently ranked higher than self-satisfaction or use of a mechanical device. So every few years the idea pops up that brothels should be made legal, and citizens who go without sex should have sex vouchers distributed to them by the government, or that young people should be required to serve a certain length of time in the sexual service, much like they do in the military. (Honest, these things were proposed in the 2010s – but only for girls, for some reason. As if women wouldn't be interested in receiving the same services from some strapping young men.)

And now we're at the heart of the matter, my dear. What's your beef?

If sex is the same kind of basic need that meat is, and the availability of sex should be made the same kind of right as the availability of meat, then we ought to have government-run sex lots and fuck factories. They should have mind-crushingly small stalls where people are put with their limbs hobbled, where they could never see daylight or breathe outdoor air and be in constant pain and discomfort and kept in unnatural positions that cause deformities so that you can easily and conveniently, without their permission, satisfy your needs. Some of them could have parts of their bodies removed so they can't harm anyone – perhaps have their teeth pulled out, for instance, to make it easier to fuck them in the mouth. Are you a breast man, What's your beef? If so, meet the buxom Roz. She has enormous tits. So big, in fact, that she would fall on her face if she tried to stand up (if she only had the space to do so).* If a visit to the sex lot results in offspring they will, of course, be immediately taken from their mothers. The lucky ones will be raised to adulthood, but, of course, the needs of paedophiles have to be met, too, so some little ones will be made use of immediately. Naturally all of the screwees in the fuck factory will be given constant doses of antibiotics because, aside from the fact that diseases can quickly spread in such cramped quarters, many of them will be lying in their own shit. They'll also be injected with hormones to give them those big tits or hefty backsides or whatever part of the body your fetish demands.

Would you enjoy sex under those conditions, Mr Beef? I think you would. You'd like it a lot. Your tiny little prick (or should I say your proggle prod?) would get nice and perky at the mere thought that they would all be just *a mass to be fucked* and that you would be their *absolute master* and for once you'd get some *no-holds-barred enjoyment*, and there would be nothing anybody could do about it.

Some people (not you, because it would be more expensive and not subsidized by the government) will want to go to all-natural sex lots where the screwees would have slightly better conditions, like taking care of their own children, not being force-fed medicines and eating somewhat better food. But they would still be slaves to the hedonism and indifference of people like you even if they hadn't had every trace of human dignity taken from them.

Oh yes, and the Catholic priests you mentioned who are driven by their celibacy to do all those unfortunate, nasty things – if you, or all of us, for some reason were denied this critical source of protein, do you think there would be mysterious disappearances of small, or not so small, children in your neighbourhood? Because what else can you do if your means of satisfying this *basic human need* is taken away?

* Roz is a reference to the American chicken breed, the Ross 508. The vast majority of Finnish chickens are of this breed. It's been 'refined' (in quotes because there's nothing terribly fine about it) to produce the maximum possible quantity of the most desired meat – the breast. The breasts of Ross 508 chickens are so unnaturally large that in many cases the birds can no longer keep their balance. A Ross's life is strictly regulated. In the feed lot the animals' daily cycle is regulated through the use of lights so that they'll sleep as little as possible. They're fed constantly. Since they have nothing else to do, they eat. In six weeks the miserable creatures have grown to weigh nearly two kilos. They aren't allowed to grow any older than that because it would make the meat unpleasantly tough.

LEAVE A COMMENT (total comments: 69)

USER NAME: No user name
This E.H. guy is looking for a punch on the nose. Does anybody know who exactly he is? Give me a hint where the shithead lives, and I know how to teach him.

SHOW ALL 68 COMMENTS

DAY FOURTEEN

I've spent the evening at the console taking notes. I had to drive all the way to Tampere because I couldn't get everything I needed at the village store. Some of the items were hard to find.

I read on the net that black velvet is the best material for lining the box because it doesn't reflect light at all. I glue the pieces of velvet to the inside in strips and construct a tight, velvet-lined, removable cover.

You need the thinnest possible material for the pinhole. If you just make a pinhole in the side of a box that's made of something thick like corrugated cardboard, it will scatter the light. I find a tip that says the thicker aluminium foil from the supermarket works well if you just remember to blacken the inside with a matte finish using the soot from a candle flame.

I make the shutter out of a thickish piece of black rubber attached to the outside over the hole. The rubber fits tight against the hole and the side of the box. I rig it with a wire hook to tug the flap away from the hole and control the exposure.

I've bought real photographic paper and developer and stop bath and vinegar and three shallow plastic pans and a red darkroom light. Port of Departure's regular photographer, who helped me locate some of the hard-to-find items, suggested that photographing directly on to paper would be simplest.

This camera will have absolutely no electronic components in case that's the key.

At first I notice that although I can see the opening in the hayloft wall there's no reflected image of the landscape on the back wall of the camera when I try it out. I don't let this discourage me because I've gone to a lot of trouble to build the thing. I change the position of the camera and come up empty again. Then it occurs to me to put the box on the old kitchen stool from the junk room, with the front wall of the camera right next to the opening.

Now I can see it.

Finally. My stomach tingles with triumph and excitement.

The Other Side shows on the paper as a tiny, amazingly sharp, upside-down, detailed image.

I go through almost half a pack of photographic paper with no success. I know in principle, from the instructions I found, to count the time the shutter's left open, but to calculate the right exposure I would need a light meter, and I don't have one. I try just counting the seconds of different exposure times in my head.

It's a task that takes an excruciatingly long time because after each exposure I have to carry the box down the ladder and over to the cellar under the cottage, where I've built a work table out of produce crates and plywood, then turn on the darkroom light, use tongs to rinse the exposed paper in developing fluid and wait to see if anything appears. It's also hard to judge the results because the paper creates a negative, black-and-white image, so a very bright image is badly underexposed and vice-versa. Most of them are underexposed. I obviously don't have the patience to hold the shutter open long enough.

When I gradually begin to believe that I've nearly got it right I realize that the evening is starting to get dark.

I can't take any more pictures today.

The funeral's tomorrow.

PERFECTING THE HUMAN SPECIES
A BLOG ABOUT THE ANIMALIST REVOLUTIONARY ARMY
AND ITS ACTIVITIES

A REQUEST FOR HELP

Can anybody rake up some muck for me about beef production? I have quite a bit of dirt already, but more wouldn't hurt. Beef cattle is of particular interest to me at the moment. Production maximization.

LEAVE A COMMENT (total comments: 31)

USER NAME: JesseP

You find all kinds of stuff in the US these days. The use of hormones and antibiotics is old news, of course. Both the hormones and the antibiotics can be transferred to humans, which has happened in the United States among other places. Hormones are particularly dangerous for children because they can cause puberty to start years ahead of time. The reckless use of antibiotics has caused a steady increase in resistant super-bacteria that are entirely unaffected by even the strongest drugs. The way antibiotics are being used, on humans as well as animals, is like starting a forest fire to kill a little bug — it will kill the bug, but all the beneficial bacteria are killed in the process. And if resistant bacteria are left behind an unbelievable ecological niche is available for them to fill, reproducing and spreading through excrement and other means to the whole environment. Artificial meat production

is a significant cause of the misuse of antibiotics. You might already be biting into some meat
that has antibiotic resistant bacteria living in
it, and it might very well come from Finland. EU
inspectors can't necessarily find every little
trace of antibiotic in meat.

MODERATOR: E.H.

Solid! There's a kind of cosmic justice in the fact
that humanity's reward for its unending hedonism
would come in this form. Our animal slaves
nurturing their vengeance within them. It's like a
sci-fi movie. :-)

USER NAME: Simo K.

Feeding cattle offal to cattle — forced cannibalism, in other words — was a common practice in
the United States, but it wasn't widely known until
British meat producers who used the same practice
were struck by hoof and mouth disease in 2001. Does
anybody remember that? It's good dirt, even if it
is a bit old.

USER NAME: Suzy

This is old dirt, too, but pretty choice. The USDA,
which is the United States Department of Agriculture, did some other interesting experiments on
cows aside from feeding them the bodies of members
of their own species. Some cows were given plastic
pellets instead of grass to eat. Cows' digestive
systems need non-digestible material, after all,
which they normally get from the fibre in grass and
hay. But a cow fattens up faster if you feed them soy
or grain feed, which means that buying, transporting
and storing hay is just an extra expense for the
producer. By feeding the cows plastic you avoid

having to buy hay. This brilliant plan also made it possible to recover some of the plastic from the cows' manure and still more from their organs after slaughter and then feed it to the cows again. The USDA also researched the possibility of feeding cement dust to cattle. It had a lot of calcium in it and probably other elements, too. And let's not forget that such a diet would no doubt bring an animal up to slaughter weight nice and quick.

MODERATOR: E.H.
I was going to put a smile on this one, but I can't do it.

USER NAME: Tirsu
Let them tell you themselves.
I can't bring myself to write something so cruelly ironic, so I'm just going to copy this quote from an actual beef producer's website. The title is 'Converting to an All-In All-Out Production System':
'In an all-in all-out production system calves are brought to an empty compartment and raised to slaughter weight. The compartment is then completely emptied, washed, disinfected and allowed to dry before a new production unit is brought in.
'All-in all-out can be achieved in an entire production facility or can be used in individual lot units. Use in individual units cannot prevent the spread of diseases from one unit to another but does have distinct advantages over continuous production.
'The first culling can be completed more quickly when cows come to slaughter weight. In addition to slaughter-ready animals weak individuals that shouldn't be fed to normal weight can also be sent to slaughter. The cull can make more space available for the remaining animals. The last cows can

be sent to slaughter approximately one month after the first culling.

'The emptied lot is washed, disinfected and allowed to dry. Necessary repairs to buildings can also be made at this time. The lot is ready to take another batch of calves about one to three weeks after emptying, depending on the situation.

'In an all-in all-out unit all the calves are roughly the same age. This makes it possible to optimize feed according to age. All-in all-out also prevents diseases from spreading from one age group to another. Health maintenance is made simpler and more efficient when needed treatments can done to the entire herd at the same time. Infectious diseases such as salmonella, ringworm, respiratory infections, parasitic infections and foot-and-mouth disease can be contained in one unit.

'All-in all-out can significantly increase the animal mass at the final stage of production. This increases the ventilation demands. Dividing facilities so that infections don't automatically spread from one unit to another can also lead to increased profits in many lots.'

USER NAME: Smart Alex
We don't treat animals humanely because they're not human. We do other people because they are human. The difference between cannibalism and omnivorism is clear, both ethically and scientifically. We ought to be focused on the fact that in many countries people face hunger and live in really terrible conditions, and soulless animals who don't even know anything better aren't the first thing we ought to be worrying about.

SHOW ALL 22 COMMENTS

DAY FIFTEEN

I'm already dressed in my black suit as I climb up to the loft one more time with my pinhole camera.

The queen is in the bag against my chest. The dew is gleaming on the Other Side, slanting August light strikes the trees, bushes and tufts of grass form intricate mosaics in the shadows.

To get a decent picture feels more important than ever. I can show it to someone, as if in passing, mention that I'm learning to use a pinhole camera, which would be reason enough to show it to someone, maybe an acquaintance I run into at the grocers. There's nothing unusual in the photograph; the date palms and olive groves aren't visible in it. It's just a Finnish forest. I can watch their response, see what they say. If it's just my brain making an image on the paper, if someone else sees nothing but a timber wall, I'll know what I'm dealing with.

I place the box on the kitchen stool and lift the shutter. I stare at my watch and count the seconds in my mind. When I get to forty five I let the rubber spring back over the hole.

I take the camera into the house because there's no time to develop any more photographs; it's too late in the morning. But the exposure will be safe in the dark box, a dream lying latent there.

The memorial is held in the chapel, although Eero was no more a churchgoer than I am. It's just simpler to arrange everything according to pre-existing logistics and routines. Eero is to be cremated, the coffin moved along rails through the curtain and into the crematory. Pupa and Grandma are buried at Kalevankangas cemetery, but we secular family members haven't taken the trouble to find a burial plot. It seemed much too early, unnecessary. Until now.

As I get out of the car in front of the chapel I see someone in a broad-brimmed hat who looks vaguely familiar climbing awkwardly out of a taxi. It takes me a moment before I realize that it's Marja-Terttu. She's gained weight and grown older, but then so have I. Jani isn't with her – and why would he be? Eero was just a sniffling, pink obstacle to the progress of their relationship. The driver helps Marja-Terttu take a largish flower arrangement out of the back seat. Pink carnations and white lilies attached to a split-leafed philodendron with an overly decorative gold-edged ribbon.

I should have taken care of the flowers myself. It's tasteless, effeminate, a product of her Australian tastes. I also could have got a substantial discount from my regular florist, but Marja-Terttu insisted, said I should at least let her participate in the arrangements in some small way.

Marja-Terttu sees me and looks at first like she's trying to decide, is that Orvo? It must be Orvo, and she hands the flowers to the taxi driver and comes towards me, holding her arms out a little like she wants to hug me. I deliberately misunderstand and hold out one hand, my right hand, and we shake. We don't know what to say to each other.

Can you say, my condolences, when both people are facing exactly the same loss?

Her coming to the funeral is an unnecessary gesture, almost a farce. And the farce continues when the cab driver comes over with the flower arrangement and thrusts it at her, saying, 'I've got to get going,' and she thanks him and apologizes in a trembling voice.

She thrusts the flowers at me in turn. 'I ordered them to be from both of us, like we agreed,' she says, and then, with surprising natural-ness, takes my arm and starts pulling me towards the chapel.

She probably didn't dare to stay away; it would have been too cold. Her correspondence has been sporadic – a card on birthdays and Christmas when Eero was little, sometimes a gift, too, which was nearly always something bright-coloured and noisy. Toys made in Hong Kong and broken the day after Christmas. After that there were just birthday cards, cards that even at a distance showed that her restrained Scandinavian aesthetics had long since dissolved in the land of the nouveau riche – childishly garish with two verses of some syrupy sentiment printed in gold on the inside. And a few equally garish-looking Australian dollars tucked in it.

The first person I see in the chapel is Ari.

What the hell is he doing here? There's no need for pall-bearers, especially not if they're the people who put the contents in the coffin. I would turn and leave, but Marja-Terttu's grip on my elbow is as inescapable as a ball and chain.

Ari sees me and starts towards me decisively, a carefully constructed expression on his face – condolences, solicitude, perhaps even something like manly regret. I notice that I'm shaking.

Ari stands in front of me and reaches out his shovel hands. 'Son, son!' he sighs dramatically, preparing to enclose us both in a consoling patriarchal embrace.

I push him away with such violent contempt that his wall of a body staggers backwards, and he no doubt reads the rest from my face.

I wrench myself away from Marja-Terttu's grip, turn and go to sit as far away as possible from Ari. I can hear the nervous tapping of heels as Marja-Terttu follows me. Perhaps she's sensed that there's no use trying to sort it out with Ari.

Through forest land, a travelling child, an angel his heavenly guide.
His journey is long, his home out of sight, but an angel is there by his side.

I chose the song almost blind. Hellén and Hannikainen's simple classic. It's a song composed specifically for a child's funeral, and this is a child, my child, in spite of his actual age. There's nothing in the song about God, just a wise, able, winged protector.

The song is being played on the organ, wordless. Hearing the sentimental lyrics echoing in my head is hard enough.

When the organ music ends – *Oh, little child, don't ever let go of the hand of that angel who cares for you so* – I'm supposed to get up and carry our joint flower arrangement up to the coffin, but there's a lump the size of a shoe-box in my throat.

I can't do it. It's too final. I've already given my message to Eero, a last message, a token, a guide. An angel to lead him home.

A stupid, insane, glimmer of hope.

Marja-Terttu is sitting beside me in a too-new, too-stiff suit, too tanned for a Finn, too made-up for a funeral, a handkerchief clutched tightly in her hand. I touch her shoulder, and when she lifts her red-rimmed eyes, surprised, I almost shove the too-large, too-sweet flowers at her, get up, stumble out of the chapel, my vision blurred by a wavering film that's building up, and I find my car, get in and speed away with a loud screech, leaving tyre marks on the asphalt.

Marja-Terttu left me the same way she had come into my life – determined, without bending to expectations or listening to dissenting opinions, without a glance at what she left behind or cast aside, like a seventy-kilogram force of nature. She had found me, bizarrely enough, at Port of Departure where she'd come to support a friend who was buying a coffin for her deceased father (I still remember that her friend Raakel's father had died of an intestinal obstruction, the kind of insignificant detail that my mind preserves in spite of the fact that the greater part of our marriage is oddly hazy to me). Marja-Terttu said later that she had read me wrong, that the calm, manly way I treated Raakel's grief, with the right combination of intimacy and distance, seemed to her to be a sign of inner harmony and integrity (she used words like that – she was an English-language teacher, after all), to show the tranquillity of my mind, the beauty of my psyche – but she had been wrong about all of it. She hadn't realized how carefully controlled an undertaker's persona has to be, how practised and refined it is, how it's just a surface. Sniffing out death like a bomb-disposal dog.

Didn't it ever occur to her that there must be something wrong with me? After all, I was over thirty and still unmarried. Maybe her own biological clock was ticking so loud that it drowned out the time bomb ticking inside of me – or what she imagined was a time bomb;

she never found anything destructive or explosive in me. Just one disappointment after another. One more harsh, faded and ugly matryoshka doll inside the next.

One disappointment, one of the first, was in bed. Maybe some whiskered analyst could have dug up childhood memories and their possible resultant traumas, with a knowing glint of self-satisfaction in his eyes when I talked about the bridal flight of bees, the new queen's departure from the hive, the swarm of greedy drones behind her, all of them wanting to erupt inside that mysterious giver of life and become the progenitor of a new colony, and Pupa calmly telling me how it didn't end well. Once they fertilize the queen their penises break off inside her – snap! – and the males lie dead on the ground. The wages of sex is death.

Even I don't know what to think about it. I did have girlfriends, experiments, panting and fumbling, damp and bewildered under a blanket, body parts that had been just pictures and fantasies suddenly under my fingers, sometimes a feeling almost of satisfaction, the zing of pleasure as the girl let out a sound at the right moment. Those moments were like a movie or a book and so they felt right.

Marja-Terttu thought for a long time that she could peel away my awkwardness, my shyness, probably thought at first that they were endearing qualities, a skin that I would eventually shed, the outer shell of the matryoshka doll, a chrysalis I would soon discard, roaring and tossing her from one end of the couch to the other like a wild gorilla, howling with joy, an insatiable mate, a virgin who'd finally realized his inner carnality.

But that never happened. No matter how she tried.

I didn't love her – that was the other big disappointment. She probably thought it was love when I let everything happen. A man wouldn't let someone lead him to the altar if he didn't feel something for her, would he? But it was just that I never found the words to respond to her step-by-step progression of logical suggestions. Why don't we get engaged? My mother's turning seventy this summer. That would be a good place for a wedding! Hey, I got my promotion – let's have a baby! It wasn't in me to say no. I couldn't have looked her in the eye, imagining her eyes filling with tears and defiance if I refused. And it was so easy to think that now was the time, that it was, in fact, the last possible moment that I could start a family, be normal, ordinary, put to rest for good the things that people I knew might be thinking about my sexuality.

And sometimes, when we were lying together in bed, it felt like Marja-Terttu's round, pale side rising and falling was an immovable mountain range between myself and an endless desert of loneliness.

Now I'm running away from her, my ex-wife, the mother of my child, and from my own father, a murderer, and from the shell of my son.

PERFECTING THE HUMAN SPECIES
A BLOG ABOUT THE ANIMALIST REVOLUTIONARY ARMY
AND ITS ACTIVITIES

SOULLESSNESS AND SPECIFICITY

It used to seem self-evident that there was a vast divide between people and animals. That humans were without question the most advanced, intelligent and developed creatures on Earth. Period.

This claim was based on the large size of the human brain in relation to the rest of the body.

Then we were forced to admit that a shrew has an even greater brain-to-body ratio.

But never mind that. Suddenly what was important was the number of folds in the brain. This made humans once again the most intelligent, momentarily, but then a species of whale was found that surpassed humans in this regard as well.

We were starting to have some trouble with our rationale. Whether it was language, ability to count, empathy, altruism, expression of grief, abstract thought, the use of tools, creativity – pretty much as soon as something was held up as a measure of humanity some pesky scientist would go and do some tests or observations and one species or another would prove to have mastered that as well.

Organized religion is almost the only characteristic that still separates humans and animals – at least for the time being. We haven't yet observed animals having any rites of worship or behaviours that could be interpreted as such. It's funny when you realize that it was religion – the one area of human behaviour that is the last straw we cling to to justify our superiority – that created the soul. You see, the soul is invisible, imperceptible, so it's *reeeeeally* handy and airtight to claim that humans have one and animals don't.

At some point the world picked up on the fact that at the moment of death the human body loses 20 to 30 grams of weight. It was claimed that this was because of the soul leaving the body. Although today we assume that the change in weight is caused by the cessation of breathing and the drying of the body, it would be interesting to know whether tests have ever been done on a single animal.

And even if they were, what then? What if scientists one day locate the soul – if, for instance, it's shown to be a magnetic field that can perhaps be photographed? I'll bet you anything that if animals are found to have a similar 'soul' then it will be the wrong size, the wrong colour or in some other sense clearly *not as good.*

The soul, whether it exists or not, is also not the same thing as emotion or the ability to feel it. Animals are products of evolution, just like people are, and they're born with various pleasurable and unpleasurable feelings, just like people. Such feelings are often connected with the preservation of the species and are thus among the most basic impulses. It's nice to get food when you're hungry. It's good to protect your offspring. It's easier to live when you follow society's basic rules.

Many of these emotions are based on biology – just as they are for humans – and for that very reason one of the most important rights of animals is their right to live a life appropriate to their species. In fact, the *less* ability for abstract thought an animal has, the more it probably suffers when made to live in the wrong conditions. People can easily rationalize their suffering as a punishment from God or try various thought projections to help themselves to endure inhumane conditions (like making up mathematical exercises in a concentration camp). People are also capable of killing themselves and for all we know are also better at motivating themselves to do it than other animals are. If you think about it, an animal doesn't have an awful lot of ways to grasp a situation and is thus all the more to be pitied.

If an animal is a herd animal, for instance, it should be allowed to exercise herd behaviour. That is its basic way of life. Because humans are also herd animals we understand that being separated from others and having families forcibly broken up is just about the shittiest punishment we can think of. If the bond between an animal and its young is also clearly a caring one (what I don't hesitate to call an emotional bond) then separating an animal and its parent is also an extremely cruel act.

Calves, which are normally very close to their mothers for as much as a year after birth, are often taken from their mothers at the age of one or two days, in Finland as elsewhere. The Ministry of Agriculture and Forestry says in a report that the early transfer of calves reduces dairy expenses, shortens growing times and can increase slaughter weights.

Both the calf and the mother attempt to call to each other for days after separation. The lactating cow is difficult to milk because she's reserving her milk for her calf. The calf may compulsively suck on the walls of its stall. Neither will eat. They move about restlessly and actively try to get to each other.

It vividly brings to mind the primate studies done since the 1950s on maternal conflict and studies that simulate maternal rejection. These systematic torture methods drove young primates into deep psychoses.

Can psychosis exist without emotions?

LEAVE A COMMENT (total comments: 38)

USER NAME: Siru
How horrible! I think apes are so cute.

USER NAME: Boo hoo!
What the hell kind of personal mother trauma have you got that makes you get all worked up about protecting some supposed cow-calf bond? Did you get the teat pulled out of your mouth too young or what?

SHOW ALL 36 COMMENTS

DAY FIFTEEN

I drive well over the speed limit towards Hopevale. I know that my phone would be ringing if it were on, but it's not on. Funerals might be the only place nowadays where personal-data devices are turned off. I'm unwilling and unable to talk. I can see Marja-Terttu, she would have first taken the flowers up to the coffin alone, read the text on the ribbon aloud ('Endlessly missing you, Mum and Dad') and then perhaps gone outside to call me while the other guests presented their flowers.

Not that there was a long line of mourners. Marja-Terttu's parents, who barely nodded at me, a couple of distant relatives, some of Eero's schoolmates, a few of the Singers, one them a girl I'd met before. I saw their burning looks when their eyes fell on Ari, and a man from the security company – apparently there at Ari's request – gave them the once-over as they came in. Maybe the Singers had planned a demonstration at the funeral. That would have been the only good reason for me to stay – to see what the Singers could make of the situation. A martyr's death.

There they are now, next to the coffin, their heads bent but their spirits uprightly defiant. Eero is more than Eero to them.

The name Eero was also Marja-Terttu's wish; her grandfather's name. Someone once made a joke about Aleksis Kivi's *Seven Brothers,* said, 'Didn't you start at the wrong end? Eero's the youngest in the book.' But a more sharp-eyed person would have been able to read our faces like a book that said, 'No, there'll be no more ties binding us together. This one is already one too many.'

It's often said that the first great crisis in a marriage is the birth of the first child. Two people become three, a line becomes a triangle, the relationship between mother and child sucks all the energy and tenderness out of the marriage, sleeplessness and fatigue is added to the mix and jealousy of the little bundle of vampire.

Some men claim that when their wives become mothers they can no longer see them as sexual beings. A whiff of incest creeps into their relationship; somewhere deep within them motherhood means their own mother.

Other men are just drones who become worthless once they've done their reproductive duty. Their penises break off. Snap! Although we don't die after our task of fertilization is completed, something inside us dies. We're ghosts of drones, living castrati.

In any case, the feelings in our relationship were probably so small and so wrong from the outset, on both sides, that Eero's birth could wipe them away as easily as the wind blows the new snow from a boulder, revealing the hardness and coldness under that deceptive softness. Marja-Terttu started to realize her own miscalculation. I wasn't a clay tablet, a *tabula rasa* that you could press your dreams into with a stylus or carve like a memorial plaque with your own happy history.

Eero's birth made it easy to turn on the cooler for good. My own straightforward, democratic attitude towards Eero's care brought out the dirt we had been hiding in our relationship. It seemed obvious to me that I could leave Port of Departure in the capable hands of my employees at any time to stay home and take care of Eero if Marja-Terttu needed some time to herself. And, of course, she took advantage of the situation and went scenting around more and more openly, more than is normal for a new mother, while I mixed baby cereal, mashed potatoes and let my daily rhythm slide into the routine of Eero's needs.

I should have noticed that Marja-Terttu's visits to the gym, her power walks, the considerable weight she was losing on these outings, the clothes she bought and her new, youngish, often high-maintenance hair-dos were more than a new mother's need to let off steam.

Jani came into the picture with the same brazen, bulldozerish straightforwardness that Marja-Terttu had when she came into my life. Eero was less than a year old when she introduced him to me. Brought him home like a teenage girl bringing him to meet her father. There wasn't a bit of fear about it, no electricity, because the few years we'd been together had shown her that I wasn't a predator who protected his territory and his female with bared teeth, I wasn't going to suddenly become a roaring berserker brandishing fists and bread knives, not even when my wife brought home a man and announced he was her lover and she was going to marry him.

It would have been easy to imagine such a man would be a scheming Don Juan, a ladies' man who'd easily wrapped a woman approaching middle age around his little finger, but Jani was an ordinary-looking fellow with a visible paunch and a visibly receding hairline. He was wearing a light-brown, zippered leather jacket and tan topsiders. He sat on the edge of a chair and leaned forwards, his arms twisted around each other between his knees, and nodded when Marja-Terttu explained that everything was decided and settled.

I didn't even have to try to understand the reasons for the decision, since Jani was so clearly right for her, so ordinary and trustworthy that he must have been that way since early childhood. An honest Finnish man. An electrical engineer. Not involved in something weird and morbid like I was.

We two men nodded at each other while Marja-Terttu planned, explained, pointed out. She said that half of everything – the apartment, the car, the Hopevale cottage and, of course, Port of Departure, a place she'd never worked in for even one day, whose door she hadn't entered since we were dating – belonged to her.

Her demands were completely unreasonable. She had only paid for part of the apartment, not even a full half. The Hopevale land Pupa had left to me, and although it may have been half hers according to the letter of the law, spiritually it belonged to me. And Port of Departure was mine. Mine alone. But I understood that if I had to buy her out of the house and the business I would have to sell them. Both of them. Although I was successful and reasonably well-off I couldn't scrape up even half of the market value of Port of Departure.

No, we didn't have a prenuptial agreement. I'm sure Marja-Terttu had never even heard of such a thing, and if she had she had been wisely silent, and I was about to say just that when there was a noise from the bedroom.

Eero was waking up from his nap.

The three of us – Marja-Terttu, Jani and I – stiffened. This was no longer about bank accounts or whose name was on the car registration. The fact struck us all simultaneously, even Jani. This situation was by no means a simple one for him.

'Of course, you'll have complete visiting rights to Eero,' Marja-Terttu said, and Jani nodded.

All I could do was stare, her words were so black, so dark.

'Hold on. It's you who is leaving this family. You will not be taking Eero.' I almost bit the words off.

Marja-Terttu laughed in a tone that was nearly haughty.

'Do you know how many children of divorces in this country remain with their fathers?' she said.

I pointed out that just moments ago she had, quite correctly, used a very apologetic tone in explaining the situation. That she had just said that she was the one who wanted to make this so-called break and start a new marriage with Jani because she still had a few years left to have more children. That she might be planning to have more children, but I wasn't. Eero was mine.

'Of course, a child belongs with his mother,' she said.

I asked her to explain that, to defend it.

She laughed wearily and said, 'Under the circumstances, I don't see any way that we could each have him for a week at a time.'

It was only then that she told me that she and Jani were planning to leave the country. To go to Australia. To the other side of the Earth.

They'd already arranged their immigration visas, without my knowledge, months earlier. Both had the kind of education that suited the immigration authorities. Once the divorce was final and the property was divided, converted to money, they would get on a plane, and all of those small personal items that you don't want to be without even if you are starting a new life would be stuffed in a container and put on a freighter.

Small personal items.

Suddenly all of it, the car and the apartment and Port of Departure, even the land, didn't matter any more. They were money, possessions. Yes, they were an accumulation, a distillation of years of work, honey in the honeycomb, but that was the law of life. One day the roof comes off, the honeycomb's pulled out and put in the centrifuge, and the hand that pulls it out is so large that there's no point in fighting it. You just have to start over.

'By God, you're not taking Eero to live with a bunch of kangaroos,' I said, my voice almost a growl.

'We'll see about that,' she said, sure as a mountain.

I don't know whether she was waiting with bated breath for that primitive man to finally come out of me now that I was up against the wall, for me to start pounding my chest and baring my teeth and protecting my territory and my woman and my offspring like a crazed Neanderthal. But of course nothing like that happened. After that one snarl I was completely paralysed. I became even more of a limp, soggy mitten.

But after Ari heard about it he sat me down at the table in the cottage and let rip.

Under no circumstances was I to sign any forms that Marja-Terttu could use to get a child's passport. She should not be allowed to take the child out of the country until the custody was clear.

Ari advised me to find the most reliable lawyer I could. No more day care and no allowing Marja-Terttu to take care of Eero by herself. I remembered that one of my employees had a sister who had a child she took care of at home. When I asked she said she didn't mind taking care of Eero a few days a week. Ari stressed that she ought to be paid well for her work, enough to keep her loyal, and he told me to impress upon her that Eero could never be given to Marja-Terttu without first checking with me over the phone.

Marja-Terttu could be with her son as much as she liked, so long as I was there, too.

I wondered what the point of it was. The situation was impossible. Mothers always get custody provided they aren't completely down and out, and sometimes even then.

Ari smiled his broad smile, although his nerves were stretched tight, too, I could sense that. 'You don't always have to go in with the infantry. You can send in the special forces. You never know when some alert scout might get a whiff of something sweet or sour from surprising places.'

Once we'd played this strange chess game with the child for a couple of weeks I noticed Marja-Terttu becoming more hesitant, more serious, sometimes even hostile.

Then, when she was coming over to spend another evening with Eero in what was still our apartment, she said she would give up her share of Port of Departure and settle for half of the small value of the Hopevale property if she could have the car and the Tampere apartment.

I saw something in her eye that I interpreted as greed, hurry, an eagerness to end these stupid delay tactics. And if the boy was taken away from her she wanted it to be for a very good price. I guessed that the supporting beams of her new life were weighing more on her scales than one skinny little kid.

'So, she came to her senses,' was all Ari had to say about it, when I wondered at the turn things had taken. 'It never hurts to make your demands. It's not stupid to ask. It's stupid to pay.'

So I got custody of Eero.

I thought at the time that I understood Merja-Terttu's decision, perhaps better than she understood it herself.

In a bee colony, the females take three forms.

The virgin queen, the eventual queen, is worshipped for her potential – a condensation of the purpose of life, the one that every drone wants to sink his penis into.

The queen is the birth-giver and is thus above all the others, the one around whom hordes of lackeys swarm; she is the reproducer and thus the maintainer of the colony and sanctified for that reason.

And the worker bee, physically female but in actuality neuter, the one whom no one thinks of as a sexual being, but who nevertheless keeps the society going, does all the work there is to do and is treated merely as a useful part of the machine who has lost her individuality for good.

Marja-Terttu was, it seemed to me, shifting from the status of queen to that of worker (a development that doesn't occur in a bee hive, but the analogy is still apt). She had transformed from a desirable virgin queen to a respected, life-giving queen bee to a middle-aged woman invisible to men as a sexual being, whose duties are nevertheless endless. A woman who has become neuter has to do poorly paid work as a teacher, a cleaner, a caregiver, a social worker, sitting behind a counter, turning old people over in their beds, maintaining the culture by providing audiences for the theatre and diligently reading literary fiction, buying useless goods at charity sales or making useless goods for charity sales. She's the one who picks up the litter and collects the compost, who always votes, uses public transport, buys local, remembers her grandchildren's birthdays and offers to babysit so that a single mother (who doesn't yet want to give up her queen-bee status) can get out and buzz around a bit.

Marja-Terttu had in her hands her last moments to be a queen. That's why she did what she did. She obviously treated her larva with only slightly greater commitment than a queen bee, who couldn't care less about her offspring (it's reproducing that's important not its result), but above all she had to have one more virgin-queen flight, the one across the ocean.

That's what I thought at the time.

I should have known that Ari had his finger in that, too.

I only got word of it later, more greetings from the Other Side.

For me, loving a child didn't mean cooing nonsense and baby talk over the crib or losing myself in the softness of the down on his cheek. To this day I don't know what that mysterious baby smell is that women are smelling when they press their noses against the top of an infant's head. Maybe only women can smell it. Maybe it's a biological phenomenon like a bee's unerring ability to always return to the same nest, loyal to the pheromones of its own colony. My love for Eero was like finding a steel beam that went straight from my heart into his defenceless body. It was invisible but hard, unbending, an axis of inseparability that I could feel all the way to my kidneys. Here was a part of me. A metastasis of me. My phantom limb, whose pain and pleasure I felt in my own cells. When he lay curled up against my chest like a baby monkey I could almost feel him growing tiny hair roots into me.

'Orvo's a good father,' I sometimes heard Marja-Terttu say. 'He changes nappies, takes Eero out for walks without being asked. He doesn't only talk about how once his son has grown a little he'll take him to the ice-hockey.'

True. I never bought Eero age-inappropriate toys, wasn't the kind of father who gives his three-month old a set of slot cars and eagerly sets it up under the Christmas tree. Eero was a part of me, but he wasn't a mini Orvo who had to have everything that the big Orvo hadn't had in his legendarily grim childhood. Eero was Eero, sitting in his baby seat with a knowing twinkle in his eye, observant, amused. While Marja-Terttu weighed and measured him and analysed the colour and consistency of his poop like a cool-headed lab assistant, graphing the curve of his development, filling out forms, I treated him like a some-what undersized but nevertheless self-respecting, entire person. I spoke to him in complete sentences, using real, grown-up words. When I changed his nappy I sometimes politely apologized for my embarrassing behaviour. I could see in his eyes that he appreciated it and thought of himself as blameless in the matter. Eero never peed on me when he was on the changing table, although he did it over and over to Marja-Terttu. 'How does he always get me?' she would screech when once again she'd peeled a nappy off him and a clear, happy stream of pee at just the right moment shot into the air and over the changing table, with its pattern of little cars, on to her just-pressed blouse.

I would wink at him then behind her back.

*

The dagger strikes with such force that I brake too quickly and swerve the car sharply at the broad intersection I happen to have come to, steer the car on to the shoulder with the last of my strength and turn off the engine. Then I let the shout come out.

Flickering blue lights and the memory of a loud noise, and I'm running towards Hopevale Meats in the darkening evening, already night, dewy, fragrant, taking breath into my lungs as I run harder than my legs have ever run, and then I'm in front of the meat plant, and a confused scene is in front of me – the police car flashing its spastic light, the ambulance, Ari speechless but defiant, and a uniformed policeman lying half on top of someone who struggles and curses, and from somewhere far away muffled crashes in the woods and other distant, confused noises, and then there's a break in the noise, and after what seems like a long time, although I haven't even had time to ask anybody anything yet, another policeman comes out from behind the building with two young people in front of him who don't show any sign of resistance, and I recognize one of them. I've often seen her with Eero, a girl whose nickname is Tirsu, I don't know her real name, but she's not Eero's girlfriend, 'just friends', as Eero said when I asked him once, and then the policeman gets up off the grunting, spitting person, has put handcuffs on him, and I see that there's a gun on the ground, somebody's gun, I don't recognize the make, but the sight of it makes my knees buckle. 'Are there any more of you?' the other policeman asks Tirsu and the boy with her, but they both smile calmly, silently, their faces saying politely 'no comment', and the person on the ground, a man the size of a wardrobe, struggles to his knees and spits out 'I got one of them, and I'll get the rest of them'. And then, then everything comes together in my head and . . .

Someone taps on the car window, and it's like a disturbing continuation of my memory as I see a police car stopped behind me in the rear-view mirror. A cop is standing at the car door. I press the button to open the window.

'Good afternoon. Is everything all right?' the policeman says. It's not Rimpiläinen, it's someone I don't know, some kind of highway patrolman. Maybe there was a radar check somewhere over the past five kilometres. I look up at him, and he's startled when he sees my red eyes and wet cheeks.

'Not really,' I say. 'I've just come from my son's funeral.'

The policeman goes silent, although I'm sure he's been trained for encounters with human grief and anguish. 'I just need to breathe a little,' I continue, much too helpful; it would have been better to let him wallow in his own helplessness for at least a moment as a sort of revenge, but my undertaker's empathy reflex has engaged of its own accord again.

'Are you all right to drive?' he asks. 'Because you can't really stop here. If you like I can drop you off somewhere and you can arrange to get your car later.'

'No, that's not necessary. I was just leaving.'

He looks me in the eye again, assessing me, and I notice him sniffing the air and looking at my pupils.

'Be careful, sir.'

He walks back to his car and his partner behind the wheel pulls back out on to the road.

I lean my head against the steering wheel for a moment, because I know from a glance at the clock that Eero has been cremated.

JUST FOR A CHANGE, LET'S TALK ABOUT SOME PERSONAL MATTERS

Our esteemed reader Boo hoo! had a pithy comment on the previous post. Thanks for your penetrating and totally germane question! I've decided to answer it in a separate post, because my response seems to be a longish one.

Yes, my mother was taken from me when I was just a baby. And I do mean taken. Since my story is perhaps not very typical I will tell it here, although it's not directly related to the theme of this blog.

My mother lives on the other side of the world and is remarried. Our connection is a very superficial one.

When I was very little and asked my father about why she left, he skirted the issue and mentioned that she'd 'just decided to do it'. I was never given any more detailed answer about whether she was an unfit mother, or what, and was never told the details in spite of my questions. I suspected that my father was protecting me from something unpleasant. I never asked her about it because our relationship was so distant that I never would have thought to ask her. Since then I've learned that even my father didn't know everything.

Some time ago I did some detective work. I consulted a few sources and asked some questions about my mother's circle of acquaintances. I wanted to know if her new husband was somehow an unfit parent. But I didn't find anything, not even a parking ticket.

After digging through various records, I found some of my mother's former friends from university and approached them on social media through a slightly altered profile, pretending to be a distant cousin of hers. One of my contacts had been quite a good friend of hers, and they had kept in touch after graduating. Let's call her Sari.

I learned that while they were at university Sari's boyfriend at the time – let's call him Ripa – had a habit of bringing cannabis to their occasional soirées. My mother would sometimes pass the pipe around. I should point out that while such behaviour is nowadays fairly ordinary it was at the time a much more serious matter, legally speaking. The police back then might take an interest in even casual pot use.

Ripa bought his cannabis from a young amateur dealer who one day, through his amateurishness, got into a scrape with the police. The frightened dealer when interrogated, assuming that he could lighten his sentence by cooperating, had mentioned the names of some of his customers. Soon thereafter Sari faced a moment of horror and humiliation when the police staged a dramatic invasion of her home complete with the requisite dogs and other necessaries and took with them Ripa and Sari's used pipe and a couple of grams of incriminating evidence. Sari ended up in jail, and in her panic she in turn sang like a canary, giving the names of every person who had enjoyed Ripa's generosity. Everybody who'd taken a puff of Ripa's weed was hauled into court and given a small fine for drug use.

So at the time I was born my mother, a woman who on the surface seemed a blameless, respectable parent, long since graduated from college and supporting herself as a civil servant for many years, had a *drug offence* on her record from years before.

Sari said that long after she had forgotten about the whole thing my mother suddenly laid a guilt trip on her about this ancient snitching. Because, according to my mother, it was the reason that she had lost custody of her son.

Because some person X had dug the matter up. Such an insignificant crime isn't even recorded in the criminal registry, but someone who knew how to look for such things found the records of the court case.

And this person X knew what he was doing.

Person X also knew how much my mother and her husband-to-be had done to prepare for their move to another country. He must have also learned of the very strict immigration policies of the country they were moving to.

And person X came to talk to my mother and coldly announced that he intended to inform the immigration authorities in said country about her criminal record. However, he would keep his mouth shut if the custody dispute was abandoned and I was given to my father.

I must admit, person X played his role in this game superbly. Had my mother given up her plans to move and chosen to stay in Finland my father would at least have been assured regular access. It was a win-win scenario.

Why didn't my mother call his bluff? After all, it was a very insignificant offence and revealing it wouldn't necessarily have made any difference. Perhaps she would have, but because person X was a well-spoken, determined, cosmopolitan who knew how to work the system and had international contacts she knew it was a fight she was going to lose sooner or later.

I want to stress that my father was a wonderful parent, and I have no cause for complaint about my upbringing. But there is some part of me that's a bit peeved that he didn't do anything to fight all this and let somebody else do his dirty work.

And that the person who did his dirty work is for various other reasons a person that I can't in any way respect or think very highly of.

And so, esteemed commenter, I hope this answers your probing question. And now you can understand in the depths of your heart why the separation of mothers from their young is in my opinion inhumane and why I will, from this point onwards, fight anyone who does it.

LEAVE A COMMENT (total comments: 11)

USER NAME: Keijo Ernest

Fervent vegetarians see brutality in everyone who eats meat, but they're completely blind to their own tunnel vision and their lack of respect and humility about life and other people. As you can see in this blogger's writings the 'Animal Question' becomes an obsession equivalent to their own feelings of lack of love, and everything is subsumed into something having to do with 'the struggle'. 'Respect for animals' is more important than any other issue or viewpoint because it's all about justice and love and truth and everything else is evil and false . . . Experienced this way it is impossible for them to see their own ideology and activity as limited or fallible or to see the imperialism in it, an attempt to alter society according to their own desires (= a vegetarian society). To the fervent vegetarian the animal issue is ultimately more important than respecting or listening to other people (anyone who thinks differently). Let's change the world but refuse to look at ourselves and instead paint a narcissistic image of our superiority to people who eat meat. Let's worry about our values and rights as reflected in animals before we've learned to know and respect ourselves or people. Respecting other life forms has to come from people respecting themselves (and radicals recognizing their own shortcomings and obliviousness!!). People come before animals. Anyone who harps on about animal issues without understanding his own humanity and putting it first is pitifully lost.

SHOW ALL 10 COMMENTS

DAY FIFTEEN

When I get home I take my pinhole camera to the basement. I bring along a bucket of warm water. I mix the developer, vinegar water and stop bath. In the red glow of the darkroom light I open the box, take out the photographic paper and dip it in the developer.

I wait. I rinse the paper in the basin very gently. Soon I start to make out darker spots here and there and some details of the negative begin magically to appear on the paper. I can see white tree limbs against a dark sky. I realize immediately that the photograph is a success. I transfer the paper to the vinegar solution then the stop bath. I wait half a minute and the paper negative is in my hand, glossy and damp as a newborn.

I take the photograph into the cottage. I use clothes-pegs to hang it from the clothes-line in the bathroom. The plastic-coated paper dries fairly quickly, and I help it along by fanning it with a piece of cardboard. Soon the surface of the paper no longer feels sticky.

I'm a very inexperienced photographer, especially when it comes to black-and-white pictures. Aside from the negative image of the tree limbs I can't really make anything out except for some darker and lighter splotches, mere visual clutter.

I put the picture through the computer scanner and save it to hard disc. I open the negative file. I sign into the Port of Departure customer service page where I know I can find simple photo-editing software. I search for a bit, find the command to 'change negative to positive' and click.

The picture changes in the blink of an eye, and I recognize the view immediately. My eyes turn wet. There it is. The Other Side, in all its virgin magnificence, on the screen, large and sharp. There's just a little softness in the grass and bushes – the wind had time to move them a little during the exposure.

At the edge of the woods there's a vague shape formed of shadows and light that seems new, stands out from the landscape. I know that it's a natural human tendency to form meaning and create patterns from clouds and boards and branches, but, still, it makes me curious.

I click the enlarge button and zoom in.

A slightly grainy shape made up of black, white and grey, standing in front of the spruce trees. Eero.

I climb calmly down the ladder out of the junk room into the Other Side.

The evening will soon fall around me. There's still some light, but I can already smell the dew.

The birds are singing a late-summer song, no longer serenading or wooing. The sound from among the leaves is just a twittering, preparing for the coming autumn. Maybe the birds don't migrate very far any more. Maybe on the Other Side the world is gentler and milder for them. Maybe if I were a bird-watcher I would be hearing and seeing amazing things, strange calls, making incredible, exotic discoveries.

I don't go as far as the lane of date palms.

I don't need to.

I walk maybe a couple of hundred metres.

I stop in the middle of the meadow, let the setting sun warm my eyes from behind the broken edge of the forest, let the dew from the bent grass seep through the legs of my jeans to my legs.

'I came to tell you I'm here. I'm here, too.'

My voice is forceful, without hesitation.

Is that a rustling in the woods?

I turn. This is enough.

I go back. I can just barely make out the splotch hovering in the air, the suspended doorway, the portal between worlds, the ladder leaning against nothing. It will be dark soon.

Everyone else thinks that Eero has gone away for good today . . .

To a happier land.

From time into eternity.

I've basically forbidden the use of such words at Port of Departure, but right now they feel right, good, even profound.

He's following me. I know he is.

He's there behind me somewhere, where the lower branches of the spruce trees intertwine to form a tattered wall. If I turned my head, he would flash into view, the blue of his jeans, a glimpse of his red plaid shirt. I can almost hear his wary movements under the light rustle of my own footsteps. I'm certain he's taking steps exactly timed to mine, walking in my footprints with the same determination and carefulness he had as a child, walking in his father's footsteps through deep snowdrifts. His legs, like mine, are brushing the virgin dew from the gleaming silver grasses.

I can feel his gaze on the back of my neck, tingling like a sweet poison, but I know somehow that I shouldn't look back. If I look back before he's ready something might go wrong. I have to accustom him to my presence, tame him gradually, like any creature in an unfamiliar environment. He has to trust me, to feel safe following me.

Some day he'll come as far as the ladder. Maybe further.

The last languid bees are flying around the colourful willowherb blossoms, soon to return to their nests heavy with pollen and nectar.

And soon I'll return to my own world, my steps heavy with dew and reluctance.

I want to stay. I want to turn around. I can't.

But he's coming, he's following me, stopping when I stop, moving warily forward like a clever animal every time I make a move – I sense it more than hear it.

A blinding white anguish tears at the innermost part of me, and when it strikes I have to bend down for a second, inhale the cool air into my lungs.

I stand up again, panting. I won't turn around, I won't turn around. Just a few metres to the ladder leaning against nothing, the opening at the top of the ladder, the darkness of the junk room hovering there, a dark tear in the chromatic brilliance of this place, like a worn spot on a painting where the colour has been eaten away.

'Eero.' I can't help but say it.

I hear him nodding, my senses reaching out through the air to feel the hint of movement. Like the way a seal can sense the direction of a fish's movement in the vibrations of the water long after the fish has passed. I sense him like a hammerhead shark senses a manta ray hiding in the sandy seabed. He's right behind me, almost close enough to touch. My every limb is twitching to turn around.

'Eero. Is everything all right?'

I sense it again, a noiseless nod behind me. Two nods, like Morse Code in the air currents. *Yes, Dad.*

'I'll come back.'

The air sighs another nod. I take the last steps. I lift my foot to the ladder, every lift of my foot a sob in my lungs. My head is as high as the opening. I look into the darkness of the loft.

I can see the last red rays of the sunset bathing my boots in light and then I'm in the dust of the loft, and it still amazes me that there is no slant of light from the Other Side forming a bronze puddle on the floor, just the untouched dark of the room as if the opening didn't exist in this world.

Now I turn and look.

Somewhere far off, in the darkness of the woods, a flash of something – blue? red?

I only went halfway across the meadow, but there's a wake in the wet grass that leads all the way to the edge of the forest.

PERFECTING THE HUMAN SPECIES
A BLOG ABOUT THE ANIMALIST REVOLUTIONARY ARMY
AND ITS ACTIVITIES

RECOGNIZING OUR OWN HUMANITY

In my previous post I opened up a little about my own family relationships. I let myself be provoked into it because so many commenters have in the past, and especially lately, tried to find some kind of simple pop-psychology explanation for the movement for animal rights.

A favourite theory seems to be that there's some connection between motherlessness and belonging to a 'fringe organization'. Many commenters think that it's obvious that a person who doesn't want to inflict suffering on animals and fights for that idea is somehow not quite right in the head – no 'normal' person would make a cause out of such a thing!

According to these interpretations I have a need to find my lost mother in the gentle eyes of a cow, a burning desire to 'look for approval' among radical activists, I'm trying to use my self-pity and sob stories to collect cheap sympathy for my cause. Many commenters have even gone so far as to suggest that I have some erotic passion towards animals of other species (although I don't quite understand what that last assumption has to do with early loss of a mother).

First off, I'd like to remind you that not everything you find on the internet is true. My 'story' could be deliberate misinformation and provocation.

Secondly, and seriously, is it true that my concern for animals has become 'an obsession equivalent to their own feelings of lack of love, everything subsumed into something having to do with "the struggle"', as commenter Keijo Ernest so aptly put it?

'Anyone who harps on animal issues without understanding his own humanity and putting it first is pitifully lost,' he says.

*

My father doesn't read this blog because he doesn't know anything about it or about my ARA activism, which makes it not quite so horribly embarrassing to say things like this on these semi-public pages.

I don't believe I've ever experienced lovelessness. My father, who has himself experienced being motherless as well as half fatherless, hasn't shifted the trauma of rejection on to me – if he has any such feelings of trauma. My father did a wonderful job raising me, always ready to talk, to share ideas and points of view. His presence in my life has been simple and uncomplicated, an appropriate mixture of protection and freedom. He has transferred his values to me almost intact: a respect for the complexity of life, a person's responsibility to animals and nature, an interest in ecology. Through him I've also learned not to mystify death, the limit that both humans and animals must all face. If you're looking for a reason I am the way I am, look at my father – he's the one who made me who I am.

LEAVE A COMMENT

DAY SIXTEEN

I wake up to someone pounding on the door and then opening it with a key.

I sit up on the side of my bed, run my hands through my hair, my eyes not wanting to open, my heart going a million beats a minute like anyone's would who had awoken to someone invading their home, and I hear steps, then two voices, a man and a woman.

I recognize them both.

I forgot to turn my phone on.

I had other things to think about.

I pull on my long johns. I don't need any other clothes – these are people I know. I come out into the front room, and there they stand, Ari and Marja-Terttu. Marja-Terttu sets an object on the table.

The urn.

She has changed out of her mourning clothes and is now dressed in a white denim skirt and grass-green sweater. The girlish colours are too much for her weather-beaten Australian skin. I notice for the first time that Eero has some of her looks, the slope of his eyes and eyebrows, the tilt of his chin.

'Sorry,' she says. 'Ari let us in with his key. We thought we ought to come and check on you, since you didn't answer our calls. And there was this . . . this . . .' she gestures towards the container, her voice trailing off.

'Get out,' I snarl, and they both startle, almost jump. 'Not you, Marja-Terttu,' I add.

Ari takes a step towards me. 'Now, let's talk about this like . . .'

'Get out.'

My voice is so full of the authority of fury that he just waves his hand wearily and doesn't speak, backs out of the house. Marja-Terttu looks at me like she's never seen me before. Where is the pussyfooting Orvo, the man she left behind, the doormat she walked on, the wet mitten? Who is this red-blooded bear of a man?

The house goes quiet.

'Sorry,' I say. 'I forgot to turn my phone on.'

'Yeah. I brought this . . . because I didn't know what to do with it . . . I mean, because it belongs to you, you told the crematorium that the ashes were going to be placed on private property, that you have a landowner's permit, I mean you are the owner of this land . . .'

I look at the urn and nod. I'd completely forgotten about it. There's nothing in it that connects me to Eero, although I picked it out myself from my own unerringly tasteful and stylishly ecological urn selection. It's grey ceramic, manufactured in a special process so that it will decompose within fifteen years. Eero isn't in it. Eero's somewhere completely different.

Marja-Terttu gestures towards the door, indignant.

'Your own *father*! Can't you even let him . . .'

I don't say anything.

'It was an accident! A horrible, horrifying thing, but an accident! And it's not as if Eero was completely innocent of . . .'

'I'd like to get dressed.'

I turn and go back into the bedroom. I'm picking my jeans up from the back of the chair when I notice that I've been followed. Marja-Terttu is standing behind me, her ample bosom heaving, one hand bent against her chest as if out of modesty.

'Orvo.'

I look at her and it's all quite tiresomely obvious. But so what. I toss the jeans back on the chair with a smile, and with one tug Marja-Terttu's sweater is off, she unhooks her bra, I push her on to the bed and hitch up her skirt in a bunch around her waist and pull off her underwear. The act is quick and rough and careless, not particularly warm, but she sighs and moans more than she ever did when we were married. I don't know if she comes, but I don't really care that much, I'm outside and above it all, it's all just supposed to happen somehow, male and female, the queen and the drone, one more penetration of the soil that Eero came from, one more experience for her of how to become that soil, that's all.

This is her last goodbye.

We quickly wash up – after I make too much of a fuss searching for clean towels – and quietly get dressed, then Marja-Terttu gets to the point again.

'Is there something I don't know about? For heaven's sake, tell me.'

I tell her.

Ari learned a lot in America. He knew all about medications, maximizing slaughter weight, quality-to-feed price ratios, minimization of production costs through use of grated flooring and nose restraints. He didn't use any dirty tricks to manipulate the slaughter weight of his bull calves because he slaughtered them himself, and nobody was paying the difference, but if he'd sold them by weight you can bet he would have fed them lead shot or whatever worked.

He hated the EU because they poked their noses into his business with their norms and prohibitions and directives. Before the EU came all you needed to get quality certification was a good relationship with a local vet.

And Hopevale Meats had never been one of those nests of horrors that you read about in the papers sometimes – creatures half drowned in their own manure, diseased and covered in sores, gnawing hungrily at their cages. Hopevale was a clean, efficient abattoir.

Ari had the same relationship with his animals that a farmer has with his potatoes. Produce as much as possible for the lowest possible cost. There was no room in it for sentimentality. No farmer stares into the eyes of his potatoes and thinks of their souls or wonders whether a sandier soil would be more comfortable for the little fellows than a clay soil. The only thing about the quality of the soil that matters to a farmer is whether it helps or hinders his harvest. Nutrients come from a sack.

In the same way it was blessedly immaterial to Ari whether his calves were standing on grates or sawdust. If a grate system was easier and cheaper, he used it. When grates were banned and sawdust became the standard, he used it up to the very last week, day, minute allowed, put off replacing it so long as he possibly could, cut every possible corner short of endangering his business. He did it in every aspect of production connected to the welfare of the animals – the lowest possible cost, the highest possible output, the words 'adequate' and 'when necessary' interpreted in his own peculiar, flexible way, neglect that was carefully planned and only corrected if he was cited for it, making weasely, clever use of phrases in the regulations such as 'provided it does not cause unnecessary inconvenience to the producer'.

And since Hopevale was never legally guilty of any mistreatment of animals he never worried about such organizations as the Animalists or Rights for Animals. When the fur trade was finally stamped out in Finland after years of squabbling, the tree huggers took on chicken and pig farmers. It was much rarer for them to interfere in beef or dairy production.

But then that direct-action group showed up, the Animalist Revolutionary Army. It promoted itself as Amnesty International for animals, and its members called themselves Singers.

I tell Marja-Terttu that I knew quite a lot about the Animalist Revolutionary Army and its ideology and activities because Eero was an active member. And that I've learned a lot more from his blogs.

PERFECTING THE HUMAN SPECIES
A BLOG ABOUT THE ANIMALIST REVOLUTIONARY ARMY
AND ITS ACTIVITIES

THE ARA STRIKES!

I'm too young to have personally witnessed the tobacco lawsuits. For those who don't remember the events of the early 2000s here is a brief summary.

The connection between tobacco and lung cancer is well known to all of us, and smoking is now restricted to private homes. It seems inconceivable to us that this smelly habit that's dangerous to oneself and others was quite common just a few years ago. Cigarettes and other tobacco products could be bought openly from any ordinary store (!).

At some point people started to question the ethics of tobacco producers. Why should they be allowed to make and market a product that was a clear danger to public health? If a toy came on the market that had, for example, a high level of phthalates, it was quickly recalled, even though the health risks were minuscule compared with those of tobacco. And yet tobacco remained in the stores.

Finally, a few consumers who had been made ill by tobacco rose up and demanded compensation from the tobacco companies. The lawsuits went on for years and years. The tobacco companies paid doctors to testify and even present research showing that the connection between tobacco and lung cancer was not a straightforward one. They paid lawyers to try to prove that smokers who got ill were fully aware of the risks of smoking, and were thus themselves responsible for their illnesses (which was a rather paradoxical stance, considering the above-mentioned claim that the risks were unclear).

Now you may be asking yourself why a blog about animal rights is talking about smoking.

The reason is that since the 2010s research has shown clearly and undeniably that the consumption of large quantities of red meat and meat products leads to increased colorectal cancer and type-2 diabetes.

The recommendations are clear: eating more than 300 grams of red meat or meat products per week significantly increases the risk of these diseases. Our present food culture holds as self-evident that there ought to be some animal protein in every meal or it's not a meal at all. The present average meat quota is one to two times that recommended weekly allowance. A couple of slices of ham with breakfast, spaghetti with meat sauce for lunch, steak for dinner. It's quite common for a Finn to eat a kilo and a half of meat every week – five times the recommended amount.

Why don't we talk more about this? Who is withholding this information? The papers used to run regular features on how to quit smoking. Where are the articles about how to quit eating meat? (I'm not talking about the occasional vegetarian recipe, but rather articles with detailed information on the dangers of meat and instructions for the reader on how to give it up.)

Who will the first person be who rises up against the meat producers and demands compensation?

When will there be warning labels on meat packaging? We put information on cigarette packets about the dangers of tobacco, so it's an obvious step to take for exactly the same reasons. Who will be the first Member of Parliament to take the first steps towards achieving this?

How many people know that a child under fifteen kilograms should eat no more than one hot dog per day to avoid the health effects of nitrites?

I'd like to see a meat counter with a sticker on every single package of steak, hamburger and pork chops – not to mention the sausage and ham – that says: 'THIS PRODUCT CAUSES CANCER AND DIABETES. USE IN MODERATION.' And in smaller text below that: 'This package contains 80 per cent of the recommended risk-free weekly allowance.'

I think it would be so, so nice if kids who knew how to read looked at their parents with wide eyes at the store and said, 'We shouldn't eat that, should we? It causes cancer,' and their parents had to explain uncomfortably that 'Yes, but it's quite good for you in small quantities,' just like they had to explain their smoking to well-informed children in decades past. Many parents would no doubt lie, make up some clever explanation. 'Oh, that's just a lot of faddish nonsense. Eat some more stew, sweetheart.' But the thought would nevertheless be in the back of the child's mind, simmering.

Since the demand for meat would probably decrease significantly once there was more information, intensive meat production would not necessarily be needed any longer. The treatment of animals would improve and the quality of meat would increase for those who still wished to eat it in small quantities. The price would also adjust to an appropriate amount as meat became more of a luxury item.

Because there is as yet no such bill for the promotion of human health, the ARA plans to strike a blow for the cause. We've printed 100,000 stickers that read 'This product causes colorectal cancer and diabetes'. On a certain day, at exactly the same time, 500 ARA members will be at the largest local markets around Finland, putting these labels on 200 packages of meat and meat products. We will attempt to make the action as unobtrusive as possible by placing unlabelled packages on top of those with labels so that ideally the action won't be noticed until the labellers have left the store, allowing customers to find the labelled products before the staff do.

The stickers are highly adhesive, so they won't be able to remove them without destroying the packaging.

We've announced the time for the action to several information sources sympathetic to our cause. Representatives of these publications will just 'happen' to be on site at the time of the demonstration, and some participants have been given instructions to get caught in the act so that they can give a statement to the press about our message.

And if any of you reading this are representatives of the authorities, the meat industry or the retail market don't bother rushing to the phone.

Because it all happened three hours ago, and I would guess that the hubbub will be starting right about now.

LEAVE A COMMENT (total comments: 94)

USER NAME: Tirsu
    Yes!

USER NAME: Progs rock

This person is able to write his blog posts and plan his sabotage because his forefathers ate meat and grew enormous brains and used those enormous brains to develop ways to acquire the animal protein they needed. If society hadn't followed this road E.H. would be expressing himself from a tree. 'Eeee ooo ooo ooo ooo!'

MODERATOR: E.H.

I completely agree that the human body and efficient brain activity require protein. But there is no evidence that animal protein specifically is necessary. Perhaps our esteemed commenter should re-examine the adequacy of his own brain-building nutrients.

USER NAME: Shame on you

As a long-time conservationist I can tell you that the ARA has done nothing but harm. Right now organizations that are taken seriously are ending up having to continuously defend themselves on top of everything else they have to do because of these self-serving dilettantes who never think about anything other than bolstering their own egos. These people are REALLY far from nature. They're absolutely narcissistic navel-gazers wallowing in self-pity. Plus they're publicity hounds.

USER NAME: An attorney will be contacting you

This blog and the moderator E.H. have made it their life's mission to sabotage a law-abiding business sector, to spread slander and defamatory propaganda. There will always be weak individuals who go to these extremes. I just read in the *Market Times* that shares in meat production have fallen significantly in the past two years. Who will be to blame if the viability of our domestic food production is weakened? Meat producers will soon have to pass these extra costs on to their customers. What good will it do anyone if inflation gets out of control? The intentional demonization of an important field of food production is extremely socially irresponsible and calls for legal remedies. And there will be legal remedies if the present government does their job.

SHOW ALL 91 COMMENTS

DAY SIXTEEN

Marja-Terttu looks at me, waiting.

'Eero was a Singer. He lived and breathed it.'

She trembles involuntarily at my choice of words.

'I know. Ari told me.'

'He and members of his cell got a media-sexy idea. He would free his own grandfather's cows.'

'Ari told me that, too. But . . . freeing those thousand-kilo hunks of meat?'

'They probably weren't planning to free the grown animals. Probably the calves.'

Marja-Terttu wrinkles her brow.

'And . . . that's when the terrible accident happened?'

'So Ari didn't tell you everything? I'm not surprised.'

'What do you mean everything?'

I close my eyes as I speak. I don't even know what words to use, because

we're approaching the target quietly, dressed in black, not making a sound, a rushing in our veins, the August night dark enough to hide the four of us. The fence around the property is quite basic, nothing our wire-cutters and wits can't get through. I've drawn a map of every part of Hopevale Meats from memory. It was easy to visit the place on some pretext or other because I'm a relative coming to say hi to Grandpa. Now I know the indoor feed-lot like the inside of my own pocket, know how to turn out the lights, know that there's no staff here at night, know where the calves' stalls are, what they look like. At first glance they look like babies' cribs, but these are made of cold metal pipes welded together into baby jail cells packed tightly together, one and a half square metres of floor space for each cage, a thin layer of trampled straw over the concrete floor, two fold-down feeding racks attached to the bars, coldly efficient. The cages are lockable but aren't locked. The worst part is crossing the yard where we have to slip quickly past the lamp-posts and disappear among the shadows of the feed-lot wall. I know the window we want. I have the glass knife, Tirsu has the masking tape, every motion and gesture practised to keep it to a minimal number of seconds. It's silent as a grave and we don't see anyone. Somewhere inside a bull calf stamps and moos sleepily. We run, crouched down, our hearts pounding. When we get there we see the window. I nod. Tirsu hands me the tools, and then SOMEBODY STARTS YELLING and it splinters the solidity of the night and there's light light light in my eyes I can't see anything and then there's someone, two, three big men, big as hell, one bald-headed one says 'Well, if it isn't Hopevale Junior! We finally got our hands on the fucker.' How does he know? How does he . . . What's he got in his hand? Oh God what's he got in his hand? And then Ari is there even bigger behind the glare of light, and I understand as I run away and the others are running, too, scattering, found an escape route, my feet like two pistons, the edge of the darkness is right there and I cross it and I'm safe Oh God I'm going as fast as I can they can't catch me, then there's a light from behind me and a black shadow in the middle of it and there's a HIT HIT HIT between my shoulder blades as I cross the into the dark into the dark . . .

'Ari knew,' I say. 'Not just about the action. He knew that Eero would be there.'

Marja-Terttu just stares at me.

'No.'

'Yes. He got a tip from somewhere. Meat producers have to have their own channels now, moles in the movement. Having paid security or staffing the place every night would be a lot of trouble and expense if it were just a matter of guesses and rumours. He got in touch with Pro Good Life. The proggles. Promised a good reward for stopping the attack, gave them a free hand. Completely free. He stressed that.'

'Even though he knew Eero would be there?'

'He decided to teach the boy a lesson – a real, tangible lesson. But there were a couple of things he didn't know – he didn't know that the Goodlifers, especially the higher ups, had a few grudges. And a few concealed weapons. And that they had not just adrenaline but also a dose of amphetamines pumping in their veins.'

It was Ari who'd done it, run into the yard, pointed at the dark form escaping, aimed the powerful LED light in his hand straight at Eero's back, yelled something encouraging, Stop him, Stop him, and then a shot rang out. One shot, two, three.

The man who taught me to love. Taught me to appreciate things. A man I looked up to, sometimes almost worshipped. I can see in his face that he thinks he did the right thing, but he's done an irrevocably wrong thing. All I can see in his face is horror as what he's done dawns on him, as I run him down, this bull of a man who's destroyed my life, run with all my strength and all my fury, climb the wall of my father with straining limbs, a wall that was once my rock, and I let my feeble hands, used to sitting at a desk, make fists and pound against that wall of meat, and maybe I find something to put in that hand, maybe it's Ari's own flashlight, and I swing it and let if fall on the top of his head again and again, and I realize that I want to hit him above the eyes, his neck, his forehead. I really want to kill him. And I would kill him if someone didn't grab me by the shoulders and then around the neck and knock me to the ground.

PERFECTING THE HUMAN SPECIES
A BLOG ABOUT THE ANIMALIST REVOLUTIONARY ARMY
AND ITS ACTIVITIES

HELLO PROGGLES!

Some readers have asked me what words like ProGL, prog or proggle, mean, because they seem to come up in the user names of many commenters (or perhaps the multiple names of a single commenter).

ProGL, proggle, or prog are all short for Pro Good Life. Pro Good Life is not an organized group but a sort of resistance movement – specifically, resistance to the Animalist Revolutionary Army and other animal-rights organizations.

PGL's point of view is that animals are intended for human consumption – although they don't explain who or what intended, promised or commanded such a thing. They believe that it is a basic human right to eat the flesh of mammals, birds and all other animals without any restrictions. PGL sees nothing wrong in the industrialized production of meat for human consumption. They also agitate strongly for a meat-based diet and argue that humans can't live a healthy life without large quantities of animal protein.

PGL's activities are assumed to be at least partially funded by the meat industry. They also seem to have political connections to advocates for factory farming.

It will be interesting to see what kind of meat industry lobbying we'll be hearing about now that the US beef industry is starting to become desperate about bee-colony collapse. PGL, like the bloodhounds they are (at the ends of their handlers' leashes), are howling now about how meat should become a Finnish cash export.

LEAVE A COMMENT (total comments: 117)

USER NAME: Seppo Kuusinen
It would be utterly irrational from a Finnish economic standpoint to even try to drive down meat production at a time when events in the world are creating a large natural demand. PGL is doing excellent work because they are able to support these businesses, and they have the backbone to respond to the baseless claims of animal-rights fanatics.

MODERATOR: E.H.
Yeah, there's a steady 'natural demand' for weapons in the world, too, which makes producing and selling them an automatically ethical act, right?

USER NAME: Proggle pride
If you Singer propeller heads had your way we'd have quite a mess on our hands. Unimaginable suffering. If humanity gives in to Singer propaganda and terror, like having vegetarian meals in schools, it will all be downhill from there. I'll give my kid money on veggie days so he can go to the hot-dog stand. At least it's food and not fodder.

USER NAME: PRG rules
So what do you want us to do, crouch naked in a lean-to gnawing on frozen swedes?

USER NAME: Never forget
Van der Graaf, the one who shot Pim Fortuyn, was an animal-rights activist. That tells you what kind of people vegetarians are. That murder has still not been avenged.

USER NAME: Tirsu

Why not play your trump card and point out that Hitler was a vegetarian, too? Sigh.

SHOW ALL <u>111</u> COMMENTS

DAY SIXTEEN

Marja-Terttu is in a hurry to leave. Stopping by Hopevale wasn't on her itinerary. She has to go to her hotel, check out, rush to the airport; she's scheduled her own son's funeral between the two closest available flights.

She asks me to check on my console to see if her flight's on time. And it is. It left from Sydney a long time ago, has already stopped off in Bangkok and is making a wide arc of carbon dioxide jet trail through the Asian night sky where the smoke of millions of tiny campfires have already blanketed the atmosphere in any case, preventing the extra heat from dispersing into space. Or so her son has informed me. But I'll spare her that. I can at least spare her something.

And while I'm fiddling with the console – ordering a taxi now – Marja-Terttu finds something before I can stop her. I left it on the table. A printout. An enlargement of part of a photograph.

She peers at it, frowning, then smiles. 'Eero. It's a little blurry, but I recognize him. Where was this taken?'

For a moment I'm very, very quiet.

'Right near here.'

She looks at me pleadingly. 'Is this the only copy?'

I know what she means.

'You can have it.'

She thanks me, effusively, with some struggle, then makes the same gesture preceding a hug that she made in front of the chapel and I respond the same way I did then – pretend to misunderstand and clasp her hand.

She leaves.

I sit down and click over to the news feed.

The USA and colony collapse are still the top headline.

In addition to almonds America's other nut harvests have suffered noticeably from the disappearance of the bees, including peanuts, the newsreader explains and adds the somewhat contradictory fact that peanuts are not nuts but legumes. And that we should keep in mind that peanut butter has been one of the most important sources of inexpensive protein in America's poorer households.

The newscaster tries to lighten the bleak tone of his text: not everyone will mourn the loss of broccoli, a vegetable that George Bush senior famously hated and a crop whose harvests are also collapsing. He adds, apparently remembering the seriousness of the subject matter, that carrots, cucumbers, pumpkins and onions have now become luxuries in North America. As have apples, apricots, nectarines, pears, plums and peaches. Strawberries, blueberries and cranberries – including wild varieties – are also becoming more and more scarce. A few growers are hand-pollinating their fruits and getting astronomical prices for them. Pineapple, however, is still available.

We already know the fate of meat and dairy products.

The main sources of nourishment for Americans for the time being are corn, wheat, potatoes and rice. Poultry is holding steady, but there's a shortage of feed for them as well.

There has been such an unprecedented strain on fisheries off the coast of North America that the rest of the world has had to enact sanctions. The newsreader says that the tough food situation in the USA makes the sanctions possible, because if South America, Asia and Europe cut off their supplies of meat, fruits and vegetables, it would leave the USA in a worse jam than it's already in.

The focus is on food. The cotton harvest isn't mentioned. But it is also suffering from a lack of pollinators.

The newscaster doesn't mention whether anyone misses their honey.

I take Eero's urn.

I bring it to the Other Side, to the shore of Hopevale Lake.

I don't even bury it.

There it sits – grey, beautiful, shapely. It will decompose when its time comes.

The rain and wind will dissolve it.

But some day, maybe today, Eero will come out of the woods, listening to the air like an animal and walk around it like an insect around a sweet flower.

Out of curiosity he'll lift the lid and sniff at it, and maybe he'll remember. My house of clay, he may say to himself if he still speaks – in the language that once united us.

How wonderful the smell of immortality is.

He's one of them now.

He's taken wing.

As I look at the sunlit urn I know that there must be a rational explanation for all of this. Just as electricity was once a cheap magic trick done with catskin and amber and now it's an untiring servant in every house. We just don't have all the facts yet.

Evolution, that blind watchmaker, doesn't set species in motion one by one. When conditions change for one species, and it assures its own survival through natural selection, the same process, half by accident, sends other species in a certain direction. If an animal grows a long warm coat suddenly there is a tempting new ecological niche for parasites. Promoting our own survival may inadvertently open a door that benefits another species.

There are varieties of fungus that grow only in the foundations of houses. Sparrows at one time moved into the cities to feed on horse manure, and rats and pigeons wouldn't be such common everyday companions to humans if humans hadn't opened the door for them as well, a door to new worlds with more food, more ways to live than they could ever have imagined in their meagre existence in the wild.

These kinds of mutual mutations might even have been a necessity of symbiosis, a bit like a dog's ability to read human behaviour. When species start to live together they even start to share pathogens such as influenza passed from birds and pigs to humans.

Could the abilities that bees have acquired also spread to humans and produce some sort of . . . broadening of our world of perception? Some ability that, under precisely the right conditions, a human would also have?

It might not be a good thing for bees, but maybe they have worlds to spare.

I go back to the opening slowly, dawdling, perhaps hoping for some sign from Eero. But I don't want to rush it. He can make the first move himself – if he wants to, when he wants to. I can wait.

The ladder rises at a slant into the air, leaning against nothing. It looks utterly ordinary and completely surreal at the same time, like a cleverly manipulated photograph. *May you build a ladder to the stars . . .*

But this ladder leads away from the stars back to the dull, grey, noisy world, the smell of blood and exhaust.

The wasteland.

Those who are faster and wiser have already made their choice. The bees.

They've gone quiet now. Night will be here soon.

PERFECTING THE HUMAN SPECIES
A BLOG ABOUT THE ANIMALIST REVOLUTIONARY ARMY
AND ITS ACTIVITIES

ENTERPRISE PROTECTION

My blog has received a whole lot of comments about the Enterprise Protection Act.

This is very new legislation, and I assume that many of the comments mentioning it come from among the ranks of the Finland First faction of the True Finns, the Centre Party or related groups.

This law came up for consideration very quickly because there have been a large number of not just physical but also informational attacks on factory farms. Until now there was no 'real' legal means of preventing such attacks. Freeing fur animals, for instance, was at worst 'obstruction of economic activity' or 'disturbing the peace'. The new Enterprise Protection Act that some of our own commenters have lobbied for would mean that any sort of legal activity that 'obstructs a law-abiding enterprise' would be a punishable offence subject to large fines. The interesting thing about this new law of theirs is that it includes a clause that, depending on how it is interpreted, could conflict with laws protecting freedom of speech. The clause says that 'if someone purposely attempts to distribute in the media incorrect or unconfirmed information that could hamper or be detrimental to the operator of an enterprise in a given field or portray such a person's product in an unfavourable light . . .' It has been cleverly compared with the laws against premeditated attacks on people of specific ethnic or other defined groups.

In summary: 'preventing or obstructing someone from operating an enterprise of national importance without legal justification' is a crime. It would make the activities of the ARA illegal because many of the posts on this blog would be categorized as 'public incitement to criminality'.

Let's do a bit of comparison. If there were still a significant mobile-phone industry in Finland, as there was a decade ago, this law would have forbidden the mention of any 'unconfirmed' connection between brain tumours and mobile phones. A racist comment such as 'Somalis are all criminals' is wrong and sweeping and harmful to a group of people. But saying that 'mobile phones cause brain tumours', although it may not be backed up by research that everyone (by which I mean, of course, everyone including mobile-phone manufacturers) accepts, may soon also be an act of criminality.

Which means that when I say that 'animals are treated in a horrible, relentless, extremely cruel and uncaring way on factory farms and feed-lots' or tell you that 'the methane emissions of cows and pigs significantly increase global warming' or that 'eating meat is bad for your health' I'm obviously hampering somebody's enterprise. I actually suspect that there has long been a sort of code of silence for these same reasons of 'protecting enterprise'. There has been a lot less talk, for instance, about how Finland's agricultural fertilizers have polluted the Baltic Sea.

Since I'm sure we'll have to deal with Finland First and Pro Good Life for the foreseeable future I respectfully request that our ideologue friends give themselves a catchier nickname. Proggle just doesn't stir the passions.

LEAVE A COMMENT (total comments: 126)

USER NAME: Tirsu
How about Proctol? Since they're all arseholes.

USER NAME: Wellbe
: - DDDDD

USER NAME: Laiplip
Famous for their moral rectaltude.

USER NAME: JesseP
Fartland First.

USER NAME: Tirsu

LOL! And it has the methane connection!

USER NAME: Wiljo

Fartland First. How about an anagram of that? Rant Lid Sniff. Darn Finn Flits.

MODERATOR: E.H.

Hmm. 'Why don't you go home and gnaw on a dead animal, you Darn Finn Flits!' It could work.

USER NAME: Some shred of decency

This kind of slanderous obscenity and discrimination based on a person's ideology will thankfully soon be over. It's incomprehensible to me that a representative can be democratically elected to a parliamentary coalition fighting for the freedom to operate an enterprise without harassment and hen be the victim of this kind of organized witch-hunt and outpouring of negative attacks. A Finland First attorney will be getting in touch with your internet provider.

USER NAME: Tirsu

Did he say that hens are being attacked? Aren't they the ones attacking the hens?

USER NAME: JesseP

Bwahaha! Best one today! Learn to write, man.

SHOW ALL 114 COMMENTS

DAY SIXTEEN

I hesitate as I climb the ladder. I don't want to go back. I check to make sure the queen is still in the bag around my neck. I weigh it in my hand for a moment.

What a wonderful creature.

So powerful compared with us.

Pupa used to say that a bee can hear the flowers talking and even see the ghosts of plants.

When I grew up and researched the matter myself I learned that what he said was true. Bees can sense light and colour in a much broader spectrum than we can. Their eyes don't just receive and interpret colours, light conditions and the position of the sun they also have hairs that sense the strength and direction of the wind. They contain a compass and gyroscope as well as a GPS locator and radar to detect food sources. Their compound eyes are made up of thousands of component eyes with which they sense structures in their environment from optic currents and then use the data received to measure the exact distance of nectar-bearing plants from the hive.

And bees don't rely solely on their amazing visual acuity; their antennae are constantly sensing the world of fragrance. Each antenna functions independently so that the bee can perceive scents in three dimensions; they smell in stereo.

Bees can sense electrical charges in the air and feel magnetic fields.

It's pretty obvious that if there are such things as portals, doors, thin places between parallel worlds bees are perhaps better equipped to find them than any other creature.

They've probably found myriad gateways over many millennia, endless untouched worlds, and colonized them without humans.

Their own Elysian Fields where angels' blood is never shed. Immortal, forever young.

There's more to these little winged creatures than meets the eye.

The darkness grows thicker and I wait for the stars, holding my breath. I believe that even at its darkest the night on the Other Side isn't impenetrably black, its darkness never as thick as sludge. I can imagine that even on the most moonless, starless winter night the black of the sky must be transparent, stealthily see-through, so that you sense the flaming heat of a hidden summer beyond it.

A spotless sky.

Euripides' paradise. Euripides.

Whose slave shall I become in my old age? In what far clime? A poor old drone, the wretched copy of a corpse, set to keep the gate . . .

The idea suddenly hits me, rational, obvious, airtight.

Why sit keeping the gate, a drone awaiting autumn slaughter – even in a beehive the drones, those happy summer gigolos, are useless when winter comes, have their food rations taken away so they won't be a burden on the colony over the winter.

I could stay here.

Live here.

I could gather mushrooms and berries, dig some kind of cellar. Maybe plant a vegetable garden. Build a little cabin maybe, a bit at a time. No need to hurry. I could fish in Hopevale Lake, which must have fish in it in this world. I could pick a hell of a lot of dates. I could dry them. And there are olives.

Now and then I could steal some honey from wild bees' nests, asking for pardon.

I could sit at a fire and gaze at the ancient starry sky, the only person here.

Or not the only one. Maybe some beautiful evening I would hear a rustling in the woods, and into the circle of firelight would step a familiar form, smiling shyly, and without a word I would make room for him on my sitting log. Eero. I would offer him some fish roasted on the fire. I would hand him a brick of dates. We could talk in quiet voices. Get to know each other.

Maybe humanity has come to this earth, to our own familiar universe, through a portal made by the bees. Maybe they followed the bees like sharks following a boat, following a trail of crumbs dropped from above.

Red rises to my cheeks as I realize what I'm planning to do with my own little nest of civilization. To build, mould, bring domesticated plants, manipulate the environment as much as I can, because otherwise I can't survive here on the Other Side.

But what if I do it quite carefully?

Only Eero and I would know.

The secret would die with me.

I could do it.

I have to do it.

And I could always go back. I could take good care of the queen bee. I could just go up the ladder again with the queen around my neck to fetch something I've run out of or forgotten to bring. Go back in cold times to winter over in the cottage like a bee in its nest and watch how the world is getting on, if it's still around.

I would have two worlds at my disposal. The thought is inexpressibly reassuring and bright.

PERFECTING THE HUMAN SPECIES
A BLOG ABOUT THE ANIMALIST REVOLUTIONARY ARMY
AND ITS ACTIVITIES

AN INTERESTING LINK

This link will take you to some very sad but quite revealing video material from Finland First representative (and no defender of hens) Rauno Viitaluoma's poultry farm. In light of the fact that the Minister of Agriculture and Forestry is a member of Viitaluoma's party, it's amazing to see the unlawful things Viitaluoma is up to at his concentration camp. Fix your eyes on the sick and dying animals, the injured feet and wings, the aggressive behaviour induced by the crowded conditions. His chickens are bound to be tender, what with the way they've tenderized each other with their beaks.

LEAVE A COMMENT (total comments: 87)

USER NAME: Rauno Viitaluoma's attorney
  This is to inform you that I've obtained a court
  order to shut down this site and hold the individuals behind the site accountable for violations
  of enterprise-protection laws.

MODERATOR: E.H.
  Go ahead and try. This page is presently hosted on
  numerous mirror sites. I won't tell how many. :-)

USER NAME: The jig is up
  You're stepping on some pretty big toes, son. You
  won't get away with it.

USER NAME: Poor little things

you been watching too many disney movies animals are good grub and that's all they are they are raw materials if you start spoon feeding them and doting on them where will we be

MODERATOR: E.H.

I heard a story once. A boy climbed a tree. His teacher told him to come down. The boy asked why. The teacher said, where would we be if everybody sat in trees? The boy answered that we would be in a world where everybody sits in trees. The end.

SHOW ALL <u>82</u> COMMENTS

DAY SIXTEEN

Back at the house I make a hurried shopping list.

Canned goods. I'll have to take them to the Other Side in several trips – they weigh a lot. Tools, nails, wire.

A good, all-weather tent to start with, a down sleeping-bag, a cooker, lots of fuel. Just in case of emergency – I'll mainly be burning wood. Tough, warm, quick-drying clothing.

Salt, sugar, tight-sealing containers to keep rodents out.

A lantern and kerosene – or would candles be better? Maybe both. Nothing electric, not even battery-operated – of course.

How many matches will I need, or should I learn to use a flint?

Will I need soap? A washbasin or a bucket? A toothbrush?

Vitamin C for the winter?

The list proliferates, becomes endless, and I find myself thinking about money. How much is in the Port of Departure account right now? I never leave a lot of liquidity sitting around; I've always put the profits into sound investments. For Eero's sake, I thought.

Sound investments?

There are so many reasons now to take the money and run.

I click on the console and bring my bank page up on my phone.

The console opens to the news.

I stiffen where I stand, my fingers hovering over the phone. A flame of dread singes the inside of my stomach.

China. God, no. *China.*

They're not just talking about that one bee poisoning in northern Szechuan any more.

They're talking about colony collapse. Spreading like wildfire.

The sweaty professor on the screen is saying something about China's cotton farmers and genetically modified plants and pesticides and how China doesn't customarily communicate much about their problems with foreign powers, and now it's all blowing up in their hands.

Blowing up in their hands.

What else do the Chinese eat besides rice? What's their central source of protein? What has increased in consumption explosively in the past few years?

Pork.

It's only now that I realize that the professor isn't a biologist, he's an economist. It's not the possibility of famine for millions of people that interests him, it's the stock market.

Once the feed needed to raise pork is gone – and most of it already is – the price of meat and other foods will increase to unimaginable levels.

China is on its way to super-inflation. In fact, it's already there. The government can no longer subsidise prices, they couldn't even if they wanted to, even if they issued so many yuan that they had to cut down all their forests just to print them on.

And what's the country whose economy has long been inextricably linked with China's?

The USA.

China has loaned the USA so much that a huge amount of US assets belong to the Chinese.

Interest rates in both countries are rising at an explosive rate. All stock markets have been closed temporarily.

The world economy is faltering and teetering. No – it's already in a tailspin.

Both countries have cast their grasping, greedy eyes on their vassals in Africa. Somebody has to produce more food.

For years the superpowers have leased the most productive lands in Africa for their own food production. As if sensing this the African honeybee has so far been immune to hive and colony collapse.

So far.

The bees in Africa have not yet had enough.

It might still happen.

It has to happen.

I heard a while ago that the USA is trying to buy some country's entire peanut crop. Now I'm hearing that what they're offering in return is weapons because nobody trusts the dollar.

'They're getting them for peanuts,' is the joke going around. But it's not just peanuts. It's a huge quantity of high-quality vegetable protein.

The little bee – such an insignificant creature. You've suffered through environmental degradation, climate change, genetically manipulated plants, mobile-phone masts, air pollution, the carelessness of humans and slave labour and parasitic infestation through neglect.

Now you're leaving.

'Honey, I'm leaving!' you shout from the doorway.

And, as you go, you turn out the lights.

Or, alternatively, you set the world on fire.

PERFECTING THE HUMAN SPECIES
A BLOG ABOUT THE ANIMALIST REVOLUTIONARY ARMY AND ITS ACTIVITIES

Forgive me for the break in posts. There's been a lot of commotion around here, and there's more to come (you'll soon be reading about it in the papers). The ARA is about to make a substantial scoop.

Our civilization is built on the bones of animals.

But that has to change.

LEAVE A COMMENT (total comments: 2)

USER NAME: Tirsu

I can't get hold of you. Is your phone broken? I need to talk to you about something.

MODERATOR: E.H.

My battery crashed, but it's up again. We'll soon see who's all hat and no cattle. :-)

DAY SIXTEEN

The idea of moving to the Other Side is no longer a dream it's a necessity.

A war is coming.

A war bigger than any we've ever had before.

Maybe I'll have to give up the idea of regular visits between worlds. I can't risk discovery.

But what if I get seriously ill or injure myself and need a doctor? Or just get an awful toothache?

I don't like pain.

I take the list, which is now several pages long, and add the word medicine.

But there's no way I can account for all possible illnesses, and I have no idea what pathogens there might be on the Other Side. I don't want to die of some simple infection if there's a quick, effective treatment for it in my own world. In that case, I would have to pop in back here and hope that Finland is still in one piece, at least enough so that I could get some antibiotics. If anyone is still making antibiotics.

But what if I bring some kind of illness with me to the Other Side? Something as innocent as chicken pox, like when whites first went to America. They infected the indigenous population with ordinary childhood diseases and left heaps of bodies in their wake. I might accidentally be carrying some teeny, tiny pest on the clothing or plants I bring with me, something that would find a vast new habitat to thrive in.

I shove that and other things I don't want to think about to the back of my mind in a dense, squirming heap.

This whole damn thing is like that. I can't rely on anyone, not even my future self.

My future self.

As if made to order a new monster rushes into my mind from the nether regions of my brain, newborn, glistening wet, wide awake and unspeakably terrifying.

What if. What if Marja-Terttu's sudden desire for sex wasn't just a reflex brought about by the pitiless reality of her loss? What if she wanted to get pregnant?

I try to knock the thought out of my head with a sharp shake. Marja-Terttu's almost fifty years old!

But that's nothing nowadays, the monster says. Not in these days of hormone replacement and the increasing lengths of active life – and the monster's right.

A thought flashes across my mind – maybe she takes royal jelly – and I can't help but shudder.

Before I met Marja-Terttu I briefly spent time with a woman several years older than me. We went out for dinner and to the theatre a few times. She was elegant and youthful, a lively conversationalist with a quick wit. One of the things I liked about her was that she didn't have any negative reaction to my bee-keeping hobby – she even seemed to take an active interest in it.

Then one day she asked in passing whether I could get her some royal jelly from my beehives.

Mother's milk. The substance newborn larvae eat and queens enjoy all their lives to allow them to lay eggs.

This woman wanted it because she'd heard that it could increase performance, promote hormone balance, reduce stress and (she said in an insinuating whisper) improve your sex life.

I hadn't heard anything that disturbing since I'd learned that some women who are afraid of getting old take injections containing human placenta extract. I'm sure the poor woman still doesn't know what was wrong when I announced not long after that our dates would be ending.

*

But what about Marja-Terttu?

Why would she choose me?

I don't really know anything about Jani or his capacity to father a child. They don't have any children, it's true, even though Marja-Terttu wanted them so badly. But wouldn't it have been much easier for her to just find an anonymous donor from a sperm bank? Someone with the genes of a super-athlete or a genius?

But who can fathom a middle-aged woman's logic? Maybe for some strange reason she wanted to throw the dice one last time, to let me have another stab at it, literally, to try to create another Eero or Erika built from the exact same collection of genes as the son she had lost.

And what if I found out some day?

Find out that in another country practically on the other side of the world the belly of a woman once almost declared infertile had started to swell and grow. That flesh, blood and bone was about to pop out into the world one more time, the dizzying double helix of DNA, hitting me in the soul with a crowbar from across an ocean. Unbendable, unbreakable, indestructible.

A war is coming.

I feel cold. Because now I know why there are no people on the Other Side.

A war bigger than any we've had before.

Just forming the thought in my head means that despite my reluctance I'm ready to contemplate it. I'm already ready to choose. To make a decision.

Australia. With the instincts of a queen bee Marja-Terttu has escaped to the furthest corner of the world, a place that might be able to remain separate from all the horror. Where she'll raise my offspring, safe for now, and when that safety eventually starts to crumble I can ask her, demand of her . . .

The safety of my child. Another child.

I decide to proceed cautiously. Slowly.

I'll escape completely to the Other Side only when I absolutely have to. I'll wait. Listen. Keep in touch with Marja-Terttu. I'll know immediately, instinctively if she has a certain bit of news, wring it out of her by force if I have to.

And if that news comes, once that child is in the world, maybe I'll demand a paternity test.

But until then I can keep bringing the things I need to the Other Side a little at a time, just in case.

And sensing Eero's presence, the intoxicating safety of it, the revocation of the irrevocable.

I buy a good shovel, a Fiskars axe, a proper knife, whetstone and fire flint. I bring them to the Other Side wrapped in black plastic to protect them from the weather. I'll have to build some kind of temporary cache close to the portal where I can keep things.

I go to Hopevale Lake.

The urn has been moved. I can tell. I can feel again that Eero is somewhere in the darkness of the woods, waiting, breathing, almost close enough to touch.

Be patient, son. The time will come when we'll always be together.

I'm about to climb the ladder back up to the hayloft when my eye notices something behind the ladder, in the spot where the foundation of the sauna would be in my own world. A rise in the ground in a strangely regular shape, under a lush willow bush. Till now I'd thought it was just an ordinary rock, like the rest that cover the ground.

I'm curious. I let go of the ladder and wade through the tall grass to look at it. I carefully move the weeds and moss aside, wanting to put them back later just as they were, without leaving a trace.

Under half a metre of humus I find something black and reddish.

Rust. Rust and soot.

A piece of the sauna stove. And it's so rusted away that it crumbles in my hand like a meringue, and under it I find something else, the steel door, its surface corroded almost to unrecognizability. Everything I find is covered in a thick layer of black soot.

Damn. The sauna is here at some point, in the future, burned down. No doubt from a lightning strike or wildfire.

Now I know that, too.

I climb up to the loft, pull the ladder up behind me and lower it through the trapdoor into the barn.

And then I hear a voice that scares me so that I almost hit my head against the hayloft ceiling.

'What in God's name have you been doing all this time?'

Ari's voice.

Ari has come into the barn.

'And what are you doing with the ladder? What the heck are you up to?'

I can't get a word out but I have to do something, and damn fast. I climb down the ladder, my heart going like a rabbit. I improvise, badly.

'I moved the ladder thinking I would clean the junk room. Throw some old stuff down from up here.'

Ari's gaze sweeps across the bark and sawdust-covered floor.

'But you didn't clean.'

'I . . . couldn't bring myself to throw anything away.'

This makes Ari laugh, and although I can tell that he bought my bluff I can't help being reminded again that there's nothing more hilarious to Ari than other people's personal weaknesses.

'There's something I want to talk to you about. I know that you haven't been feeling like talking to me, but I think this will interest you.'

He stretches a hand out towards me. Something small and fragile is lying on his palm.

A dead queen bee.

The sight is a punch in the gut. I glance unintentionally at the trapdoor. Oh God. Oh God. I can't let him into the hayloft now, not for anything.

'I was out there walking around and I saw that you seem to have an empty hive.'

'Oh.' I try desperately to remain neutral.

'Oh,' he says. 'All these years fussing over those bugs, and all you say is "Oh". I've been following the news, you know. And besides, I'm the one who made you responsible for the Hopevale bee operation. What if this is colony collapse?'

'I just checked them a couple of days ago, and everything was fine.'

Hell, no. Here I stand, a fifty-year-old man, being scolded by his seventy-year-old father, with my head lolling, and all the while a terrible secret burning inside me as if the thing lying against my chest isn't a queen bee but a stolen lollipop.

I stretch out my hand. Try to make my voice authoritative, but it's almost hopeless.

'Give it to me. I should send it to be analysed.'

Ari clasps his hand around it and pulls back. I grit my teeth. I have to handle this carefully, damn it.

'At least come and look at the hives,' he says, turning and walking out of the barn. I follow him as if on a leash. I can't let him get away, not with the queen.

I don't even have to open the hive to know that it's silent as the grave. Dead. No bodies around it. A clear case. Couldn't be clearer.

Ari still has the queen in his fist. Ideas flood into my mind. I see myself jumping him, hitting him with my fists, grabbing something to use as a weapon, cracking his skull with it. Dragging his body to the Other Side where no one will ever find it. A brick. I just need to find . . .

But I can't do that.

I have a motive. Too much motive.

The blood would stain my clothes.

Of course I could take my clothes and the weapon, the brick or whatever, to the Other Side, wash it clean in the waters of the future Hopevale Lake. But I would still be the prime suspect. They would find traces of Ari's cursed DNA somewhere on the ground or on me. And then they'd lock me up.

I can't take the risk. I might never get back to the Other Side.

For two weeks I've been just a breath away from patricide, and now I can't do it.

'What are you glaring at? Don't tell me. I know, I know. Why can't you believe that I didn't mean it to happen? This hasn't been easy for me either.'

Ah. He's talking about Eero now.

I reach my hand out again. 'Let me have the queen. I know where to send it.'

'You're not in your right mind,' he says. 'Maybe I should handle it . . . '

He'll handle things again. The way he handled things when Eero was about to go to Australia.

If he had just kept his hands off back then none of this would have ever happened. There would be a different reality, and Eero would be in it, a different Eero.

'Give it to me.' My voice is low, threatening, ugly.

Ari shrugs, humouring me like I'm a lunatic, which is what he thinks I am. 'Hell, take it, take it! At least you'll be doing something.'

He uncurls his fingers and drops the queen into my hand.

I try not to breathe a sigh of relief, try not to squeeze the queen too tightly in my hand. Ari's already turning to leave, then he stops.

'Oh, yeah. They said in the village that you bought a new Fiskars axe at the hardware store. Is it any good? Could you show it to me? I've been thinking about buying one.'

I close my eyes slowly. Now this. I have to find the right words.

'You really want me. To show you. The axe.'

Ari tilts his head as the words sink in, and the expression on his face tells me that he realizes that he ought to shut his mouth and leave. Finally.

The queen lies silent in my hand.

No matter what I do researchers are coming.

They'll rush in in a panic with their instruments and sample cases. Ari will eventually initiate it no matter what I do to avoid it or throw him off the trail. And if I leave I won't be able to stop them.

How stupid of me.

My absence would, of course, be noticed anyway. It's inevitable that other people besides Ari would wonder where I was. I could say that I was going on a long vacation to Thailand or that I bought a cabin in the Costa del Sol, but it wouldn't work. People are curious.

A new hive collapse could happen at any time while I'm gone.

And Ari or anybody, perhaps one of the researchers he hires, will find and collect another queen bee, a key, and through some ridiculous coincidence go into the barn with it and climb up to the hayloft.

And then the Other Side will be ruined.

What if I took the hives with me? I could harvest the honey to lighten them, just leave enough for the winter, try somehow to get them through the trapdoor and over to the Other Side. And I could leave with them. I wouldn't have to explain anything to Ari, or tell him where the eleven hives disappeared to, down to the last frame.

No. I'm already worried enough about the possibility of infecting the place with my own pathogens. I can't bring along hives that are very likely to be hiding who knows what parasites and spores.

What if I took the queen out of every hive and brought them to the Other Side one at a time? Would the other bees follow?

Maybe. But I have no idea how or why a hive decides to leave. And if a colony lost its queen the worker bees would just start making a new queen the way they always do, feeding royal jelly to the larvae, and soon enough the hive would be the same as before.

I'm sure that nothing could be more welcome to the inhabitants of Earth right now than to find an entirely new, virginal, unoccupied world. How fast they would take it over.

Quick as a flash they would make an inventory of natural resources. Where are the minerals, the undammed rivers, the stretches of land bursting with ancient timber?

I remember the kauri trees in New Zealand with trunks the size of a block of flats. I may have heard about them from Eero. About how they produced the sturdiest timbers for shipbuilding in the world, ships that sailed to the ends of the Earth and spread their infection: greed. And then there were no more trees and no more ends of the Earth.

The Other Side would soon be drawn up and zoned, chainsaws roaring, excavators chewing up the ground.

What kind of strong-arm tactics wouldn't they use to get in there?

Just think how the developers' mouths would salivate over the chance to own the undredged rivers of gold and the plots of land to build villas beside them.

Would they sell the land, try to tempt new settlers, or would they make it a place of escape for the wealthy few, a new Eden for those who could afford it, and leave the rest of humanity – poor, dirty, fainting from hunger – to survive however they could in a world laid waste by others?

They would definitely come, with their puffed-out chests and their clover and alfalfa and almond trees. They would enslave those little animals again, would think of them as helpers, as labour, and never realize that it was the bees who had diligently, untiringly worked to take care of them, that the bees were the true, kind-hearted stewards of the entire world.

And how quickly it would all happen.

Where was it that I read about how they calculated that the continent of North America before the arrival of Europeans would have sustained about a couple of million people. Hunters and gatherers mostly, nomads collecting wild rice.

And how many people are there now?

There was a time when the prairies rumbled with millions of bison.

There was a time when passenger pigeons blanketed the sky.

There was a time when pollinators lived their own, sweet, innocent lives and weren't shipped in slave carriers from one place to another regardless of how many could survive the journey.

Then the thought comes to me, unsummoned, of what I just saw on the Other Side.

I breathe in so quick that it hurts.

I was in the future.

Some things had already happened, their results knowable, seeable, touchable.

It's all clear to me now. Inevitable. Preordained.

To keep the gate . . .

I know my weaknesses.

I know the risks of giving in to them.

I'm not much of a gatekeeper. I'm just a person. Imperfect, a skittish mammal, instinctively protective of myself and my offspring. A weak creature, capable of justifying my selfishness with a thousand rational-seeming arguments the moment I'm threatened with danger or pain or want. People will risk even the destruction of a whole world if it means they can have, just for a moment, everything they want.

All of the motives for leaving or staying that churn in my mind are suddenly so much noise. There's only one solution, one road. I've seen that solution with my own eyes. I just didn't want to recognize it.

I light the sauna fire.

Hot. Good and hot. I cram the stove with the birch sticks I have stacked high in the woodshed.

Then I go into the house and find Eero's old blog, the one kept under his own name.

I haven't deleted it. I notice, too, that I haven't read the last post, the one he made the day before his death. He was preparing for the attack when he wrote it.

Look, Dad. I'm dancing.

Many religions have, somewhat paradoxically, been mostly harmful to the environment. (I say paradoxically because many religions stress mercy, goodness and empathy.) Taken literally, the Bible's command to be fruitful and multiply and fill the Earth hasn't even worked to our own advantage let alone to the benefit of the rest of creation. The Bible says that humans are the masters of other life forms, and that, too, has caused great suffering. Humans haven't been the kinds of masters we expect our own rulers to be – gentle, just and thoughtful of the needs of their subordinates. The atrocities of Hitler, Stalin and Pol Pot are small compared with the exploitation, cruelty and premeditated mass murder that humanity has practised towards animals.

Perhaps one of the most delusional human tenets regarding nature is the idea of life after death, of the Other Side, a heaven or paradise where a person can go if they live right, an unspoiled world where the consequences of our own actions are no longer apparent in the environment and where, above all, we no longer need to do anything about them, we can just stroll through peaceful green meadows without a care in the world.

The illusion of the afterlife is a convenient excuse not to do anything about what's happening now. Certain fundamentalists have even claimed that the warming of the climate is nothing we need to worry about because it's God's sign of the end of days, and right-thinking people will be taken up to the Lord when the Earth is destroyed if only they have enough faith.

Belief in the Other Side is one way that people today deny death. It's inevitable, touching everyone, sad, final. It's too painful to face. So we invented life after death. In the same way we refuse to understand the suffering of our fellow creatures. We ignore the death of our very world, refuse to look at it, deny that it's even happening because it's too distressing, makes us feel too guilty.

LEAVE A COMMENT (total comments: <u>412</u>)

USER NAME: Tirsu
Everyone who wants to, leave a comment here for Eero. I'll also put up a link to Eero's memorial grove as soon as it's ready and post your comments there.

USER NAME: B-Zone
Rest in peace, Eero. You'll be remembered.

USER NAME: Rosa Meriläinen
My condolences to you in your sorrow and to all the animals whose rights Eero uncompromisingly defended. He was our conscience and our inspiration.

USER NAME: Lumorap
See you on the other side.

I write a new post on the blog under Eero's user name but use the anonymous server to do it (I've learned that much, at least).

NOT WITH A BANG BUT A BUZZ

If I had to name a product of evolution that could be a result of intelligent design it would be the bee. The importance of bees for the ecosystem of the entire planet is so significant, so essential, that it is as if they were custom-made especially for the task.

We think we have the blood of angels in us. In action how like an angel. The paragon of animals.

But if any species has the blood of angels, the bees do.

The wisdom of bees is the wisdom of the super-organism. Even I don't mourn the death of my individual cells, sloughing off from the walls of my arteries, ceasing to function, moving on in the great circle of life. What's more important is that the organism, the entirety of it, is preserved. The hive, the tribe, the society. The ecosystem.

Individuals have to be sacrificed in order for worlds to continue. Bee colonies don't hesitate to throw out damaged individuals if they don't know enough to leave on their own.

Bees – individual bees – know when to leave the nest.

And the entire super-organism knows when to leave, too, if it's forced

into a corner. It has great understanding and even greater abilities.
Whatsoever you do to the least of these little ones, you do unto me.
And by the way, I'm alive.

I put up the post. Maybe a messianic cult will be born, built on this cryptic post made after Eero's martyr's death, written on an anonymous server but with Eero's user name. But so be it.

That's how it should be.

Just so they do something.

As I shut down the page, ready to get up from my task, the console sends me automatically to the news channel. The prickly voice of the anchorman stops me in my tracks.

'The American organization Pro Good Life announced today that they have obtained evidence that animal-rights activists are behind the bee-killing phenomenon known as colony collapse. A PGL representative says that they have found plans for attacks on apiaries on the websites of extremist groups such as the Animalist Liberation Army.

'Sources claim that extremist groups have developed a device for sending electromagnetic radiation that is disturbing to bees. The device causes the bees to leave their hives and confuses their sense of direction so that they are unable to return to their colonies.

'Representatives of the animal rights activists categorically deny any part in the phenomenon, but Garrison Slager of Pro Good Life says otherwise. He says the activists' plan was to cause a collapse in US cattle-feed production and cause severe damage to the meat industry.'

Slager, a serious-looking man in a billed cap, comes on the screen, his face red. 'Apparently their plan got out of hand, and now it's caused hundreds of millions of dollars in damage,' he says. 'These people are completely irresponsible, and they must be caught and brought to justice. Their activities must be stopped by any means necessary. The FBI is investigating the matter, and more evidence is coming to light every day.'

The video clip ends and the anchor looks calmly into the camera. 'According to the FBI the saboteurs have tentacles that stretch as far as Finland. Although there has not yet been any colony collapse in Finland, evidence that activists here were aware of methods to manipulate bee colonies has been found on Finnish animal-rights websites. The FBI has requested cooperation from the Finnish police.'

He pauses briefly. 'And now for economic news. The American-Chinese crisis has opened up unprecedented markets for the Finnish food industry. Demand for beef and pork is particularly high . . .'

The remote breaks as I pound it against the edge of the table. The monitor pings, flickers and goes out.

.

As I walk along the path to the sauna, a path I've walked a thousand times, I feel inside my head how small and soft and sweaty my chubby little hand is in Pupa's rough paw.

I trust him.

I can hear his voice as he recites:

> Fly up to the moon's bright border
> Past the glowing hem of heaven
> To the far side of the sun
> Up among the azure starlight
> Sure of where your wings can take you
> Never straying from the pathway!
> When you reach your destination
> Find the ending of your journey
> Fly up to the Master's mansions
> To the home of the Almighty
> There are flowers filled with nectar
> All the balm a soul could wish for . . .

Cursed be the stupid sentimentality that mammals fix on their offspring.

I hesitate just a little then open the sauna stove door. I take out the slightly cracked wooden steam ladle, lift some glowing embers out of the stove and toss them on the floor and over the basket of kindling next to the stove. The floorboards oblige immediately and start to smoke. The kindling basket lights even faster, birch bark and papers, old balance sheets from Port of Departure no longer of interest to the tax inspectors.

It all has to look like a stupid mistake, like I just left the stove door open by accident, carelessly left the basket too close to the fire. Some embers spilled out of the stove or a fateful spark escaped, and, of course, the steam-room door was open just enough of a crack (how terribly careless of me) that the draft fed the growing fire until it eventually reached the vulnerable old timbers, dry as dry from hundreds, thousands of trips to the sauna.

The fire is soon so well on its way that I'm coughing from the fumes, uncomfortably hot.

I back out of the door, leave it slightly ajar and walk with calm steps to the house. I take a couple of quick ones from my whisky bottle.

It will be obvious that I was quite drunk when I lit the sauna stove.

The fire department, police and insurance company will have every reason to believe that the fault lies entirely with me; no need for any deeper investigation of the old sauna or the fire in it. ('His son died a while ago,' I can hear them murmur in their investigative sanctum. 'He must have been hitting the bottle pretty hard since it happened. Wasn't his own family mixed up in it somehow, too?' And somebody else says. 'Saunas. We always take a sauna, and we always take a drink. I can't remember a burned-down sauna that didn't belong to a man in some kind of crisis.')

Ari will finally testify and say, 'He was as mixed up as a cuckoo clock, poor man.'

As I'm swigging down a third, larger glass of whisky I can see the red fringe of the fire through the window out of the corner of my eye.

Colourful flashing lights outside the window, just like before, only two weeks ago. Christmas. Christmas is here again.

The whisky isn't just play-acting; it numbs the worst turns of the dagger inside me.

I watch from the quiet safety of the house a few hundred metres away as a little tongue of flame darts in and out of the sauna window like the mouth of a satisfied cat. I wait until I can see for certain that the flames have reached through the ceiling. I know that once the fire reaches the attic it will start a cross draft and the flames will sweep through the loft and consume the whole building. The junk room is full of flammable things – the cans of paint, the old bee suit stiff with honey.

Now I can make the phone call.

When the fire department arrives there's nothing to be done. The flames reach halfway to the sky. I don't try to hide the whisky, now and then taking a stumbling drink and keep repeating flimsy explanations, inventing contradictory causes for the fire.

The fire fighters restrict themselves to protecting the nearby buildings, keeping an eye on the roof of the house.

When they've left and the sauna and barn are just a pile of charred timbers, broken glass and twisted metal, with the blackened chimney, stove and a fragment of the wall in the centre like some kind of monument, I look out at a spot about three metres above the ruins.

I have two queen bees. The one around my neck and the one Ari gave me in my pocket.

There, on the Other Side – like here – it's nearly sunset. But there's no knowing what the weather is like over there. If it's grey or cloudy, you wouldn't necessarily see anything, but . . .

If I look just right, if I really want to see it, I can.

Up in the air, an opening, glimmering. It's hovering there, only visible from the slightly different colour of the air, the light of the setting sun on the Other Side. It's like a microscopically thin reflective film or like the sunlight striking the surface of water. Something no one would ever notice if they didn't know to search, know what they were searching for, how to look from just the right angle.

And it can't be seen without a queen from an abandoned beehive.

I take both queens out and drop them on a leaf of plantain weed. I can't tell if the gesture is a tender one. It is definitely respectful.

When I look up, the air is just air again. Without any openings. A logical, ordinary Finnish August sky, bitter with the smell of smoke.

The whisky hums, my head sings.

I left Eero the shovel, the new axe, a good knife, whetstone and flint.

Not everybody gets such good supplies for life.

Maybe another door will open to Eero's Other Side some day, somewhere.

Maybe Eero will go to investigate his world and will one day smell a campfire, and there sitting on a fallen log will be a girl his own age eating blueberries from her hand.

Maybe everything will start from the beginning again.

I close my eyes. I don't know if the thought is comforting or unbearable.

I hear the faint bellows from Hopevale Meats as some bull calf with a healthy attitude puts up a resistance.

With that inspiration I lift my sturdy-soled shoe, put it down over the tiny forms of the queen bees and rub, twisting and crushing the fragile creatures with the bottom of my foot until I'm sure they're nothing but dust.

I still have one more thing to do.

I invite the cold in, welcome the ice-bright, sterile calculation. I have half my father's blood in me after all. I invoke it to guide my feet, hands and brain.

I must carry out my efficient, emotionless killing plan.

I know what I need.

I find everything at the village store. Black bin bags. Several metal spray cans of the most effective, wide-spectrum product available.

Soon I'm walking between the hives like an efficient mass murderer, like a calm, deliberate commandant at Auschwitz. The black casings lower over the unsuspecting creatures. There's no escape. Just a cloud of permethrin and it's all over.

I let the dark stench from the ruins of the sauna surround me for a moment. It's true what they say. Smoke can sometimes make even a hard man cry.

END NOTE

All of the reports in this text concerning the colony collapse phenomenon were, at the time of writing (summer 2011), authentic and accurate. The biological and mythological information about bees is also based on factual sources. Some of the discussions concerning animal rights are based on actual internet discussions.

Warm thanks to the Finnish Cultural Foundation for their support for this work.

The following works have served as sources:

Alison Benjamin and Brian McCallum, *A World Without Bees*, London: Guardian Books, 2008

William Longgood, *The Queen Must Die And Other Affairs of Bees and Men*, New York and London: W.W. Norton and Company, 1985

Hilda M. Ransome: *The Sacred Bee in Ancient Times and Folklore*, Mineola, NY: Dover Publications, 2004

Suomen kansan muinaisia loitsurunoja (*Magic Songs of the Ancient Finns*), Helsinki: Salakirjat, 1880/2008

Michael Schacker: *A Spring Without Bees: How Colony Collapse Disorder Has Endangered Our Food Supply*, Guildford, CT: The Lyons Press, 2008

Jürgen Tautz: *The Buzz about Bees: Biology of a Superorganism*, Berlin: Springer Verlag, 2009

The text includes excerpts from:

Elias Lönnrot, *The Kalevala*, translated by W.F. Kirby, London: Everyman's Library, 1915

Euripides, *Hippolytus*, translated by S.G. Gabha

Euripides, *The Trojan Women*, translated by Edward P. Coleridge, London: George Bell & Sons, 1906

Immi Hellén, 'Enkeli ohjaa' ('The Guardian Angel'), from the collection *Lasten runokirja: Suomen pojille ja tytöille omistettu*, translated by Lola Rogers, Jyväskylä: Valistus, 1930

Also published by Peter Owen

NOT BEFORE SUNDOWN
Johanna Sinisalo

PB 978-0-7206-1350-6 • 240pp • £9.99 / EPUB 978-0-7206-1591-3
MOBIPOCKET 978-0-7206-1592-0 / PDF 978-0-7206-1593-7

'A sharp, resonant, prickly book that exists on the slipstream of SF, fantasy, horror and gay fiction.' – Neil Gaiman

'Chillingly seductive' – *Independent*

'A punk version of *The Hobbit*' – *USA Today*

A young photographer, Mikael, finds a small, man-like creature in his courtyard: a troll, known from Scandinavian mythology as a demonic wild beast, a hybrid like the werewolf, and supposedly extinct. Mikael takes him home but soon discovers that trolls exude pheromones that smell like Calvin Klein aftershave and have a profound aphrodisiac effect on all those around him. But what Mikael and others who come into contact with the troll fail to learn, with tragic consequences, is that the troll is the interpreter of man's darkest, most forbidden desires.

A bestseller in Finland and translated into twelve languages *Not Before Sundown* (*Troll: A Love Story* in the USA) is a multi-award-winning novel of sparkling originality and a wry, peculiar and beguiling story of nature and man's relationship with wild things and of the dark power of the wildness within us.

Also published by Peter Owen

BIRDBRAIN
Johanna Sinisalo
PB 978-0-7206-1343-8 • 240pp • £9.99 / EPUB 978-0-7206-1382-7
MOBIPOCKET 978-0-7206-1383-4 / PDF 978-0-7206-1385-8

'*Birdbrain* is a graphic examination of two very different people and a harrowing allegory of humankind's problematic relationship with the planet.' – *Guardian*, a *Guardian* Book of the Year 2010

'A lyrical and occasionally sinister odyssey second only to making one's own foray into the wilderness' – *Publishers Weekly*

From the author of *Not Before Sundown* (a.k.a. *Troll: A Love Story*) this is a compelling exploration of the desire of tourists to conquer the world's last remaining pristine landscapes. A young Finnish couple – sports enthusiast Jyrki and his girlfriend Heidi – go on the hiking trip of a lifetime in Australia, Tasmania and New Zealand with Conrad's *Heart of Darkness* in their backpacks and the intention of being ecologically aware. As they attempt increasingly challenging trails their trek develops a sinister aspect as unsettling incidents occur. Belongings disappear and – more mysteriously – reappear. Finally the couple sense that, rather than these being random events, they are at the mercy of untamed natural forces directed by an intelligent being. The novel reveals the darker side of the explorer's desire: the insatiable need to control one's environment, to invade and to leave one's mark on the landscape. But what happens when nature starts to fight back?

Also published by Peter Owen

THE YEAR OF THE HARE
Arto Paasilinna

PB 978-0-7206-1277-6 • 160pp • £8.99 / EPUB 978-0-7206-1575-3
MOBIPOCKET 978-0-7206-1576-0 / ISBN 978-0-7206-1577-7

'Rarely do reviewers come upon a novel they believe to be a masterpiece, which they feel will become part of their imaginative lives. For me, *The Year of the Hare* is such a work.' – Paul Binding, *Independent*

'No wonder the French have made this book into a cult. Finnish wit is as sharp as the Arctic weather.' – *Mail on Sunday*

Vatanen, a journalist, is burnt out and sick of the city. One evening his car hits a young hare on a country road. He leaves the car and goes in search of the injured creature. The incident changes Vatanen's life, as he decides to break free from the constraints of his world. He quits his job, leaves his wife, sells his possessions and sets out to travel the Finnish wilderness with his newfound friend. The adventures take in forest fires, pagan sacrifices, military war games, killer bears and much more.
Now considered a classic of modern Finnish literature, this enchanting best-seller has been translated into French, German, Italian, Swedish, Greek and Hungarian and filmed twice, once in Finland and a more recent French-language production.

Peter Owen Publishers, 81 Ridge Road, London N8 9NP, UK
T + 44 (0)20 8350 1775 / F + 44 (0)20 8340 9488 / E info@peterowen.com
www.peterowen.com / @PeterOwenPubs
Independent publishers since 1951